ERNST JÜNGER

BETWEEN THE GODS & THE TITANS

ALAIN DE BENOIST

Edited by
GREG JOHNSON

Translated by
GREG JOHNSON & F. ROGER DEVLIN

Middle Europe Books
Budapest
2022

Cover image: Rudolf Schlichter, *Ernst Jünger*, 1937

Cover design by Kevin I. Slaughter

Published in Hungary by Middle Europe Books, Kft.
www.MiddleEuropeBooks.com

Hardcover ISBN: 978-1-64264-192-9
Paperback ISBN: 978-1-64264-193-6

CONTENTS

EDITOR'S NOTE

When I first read Alain de Benoist's essays on Ernst Jünger, I felt I had found the introduction I had been seeking. Benoist understands Jünger's vast body of work in the context of the Great War and the Conservative Revolutionary movement that followed. But Benoist offers more than a scholarly survey of the history of ideas. Benoist actually knew Jünger as a man. As Benoist points out, Jünger has generally been liked by those who misunderstood him and disliked by those who understood him. Benoist is thus almost unique in that he both understands and likes Jünger, his understanding feeding his affection and his affection deepening his understanding.

I want to thank Alain de Benoist for making this book possible. His accessibility—including prompt correspondence—and his generosity of spirit are exemplary. I also wish to thank F. Roger Devlin for his help with the translation. We each translated about half of the book, and we checked one another's work. I also wish to thank Collin Cleary for his meticulous copy editing, J.B. and James O'Meara for their proofreading, and James O'Meara and Alex Graham for their work on the Index. Finally, I wish to thank Kevin Slaughter for his splendid design work.

Budapest,
July 12, 2022

THE FIGURE OF THE WORKER
BETWEEN THE GODS & THE TITANS*

Armin Mohler, author of the classic *The Conservative Revolution in Germany, 1918–1932*, wrote of Ernst Jünger's *The Worker* (*Der Arbeiter*)[1] and the first edition of *The Adventurous Heart* (*Das abenteuerliche Herz*): "To this day, my hand cannot take up these works without trembling." Elsewhere, describing *The Worker* as an "erratic bloc" in the midst of Jünger's works, he states: "*The Worker* is more than a philosophy, it is a work of poetry."[2] The word is apt, above all if we admit that all true poetry is foundational, that it simultaneously captures the world and unveils the divine.

A "metallic" book—one is tempted to use the expression "storm of steel" to describe it—*The Worker* indeed possesses a genuinely metaphysical quality that takes it well beyond the historical and especially political context in which it was born. Not only did its publication mark an important day in the history of ideas, it provides a theme of reflection that runs like a hidden thread throughout Jünger's long life.

---

* Alain de Benoist, "Ernst Jünger: La Figure du Travailleur entre les Dieux et les Titans," *Nouvelle Ecole* 40 (September–October 1983), pp. 11–61.

[1] Ernst Jünger, *Der Arbeiter: Herrschaft und Gestalt* (*The Worker: Dominion and Form*) (Hamburg: Hanseatische Verlagsanstalt, 1932). Page numbers cited parenthetically in text. In English: *The Worker: Dominion and Form*, ed. Laurence Paul Hemming, trans. Bogdan Costea and Laurence Paul Hemming (Evanston, Ill.: Northwestern University Press, 2017).

[2] Preface to Marcel Decombis, *Ernst Jünger et la "Konservative Revolution"* (Paris: GRECE, 1975), p. 8.

I.

Ernst Jünger was born on March 28th, 1895, in Heidel-berg.[3] Jünger went to school in Hanover and Schwarzen-berg, in the Erzgebirge, then in Brunswick, and finally in Hanover again, as well as at the Scharnhorst Realschule in Wunstdorf. In 1911 he joined the Wunstdorf section of the *Wandervogel*.[4] That same year he published his first po-

---

[3] The son of Ernst Georg Jünger (1868–1943), a chemist and assistant to research chemist Viktor Meyer. He had one sister and five brothers, two of whom died very young.

[4] In 1901, a Right-wing student named Karl Fischer organized the students at the gymnasium of Steglitz, near Berlin, into a movement of young protesters with idealistic and romantic tendencies, to whom he gave the name "Wandervogel" ("birds of passage"). This movement, subsequently divided into many currents, gave birth to the *Jugendbewegung* (Youth Movement) and became widely known. In October 1913, the same year Jünger joined, the Youth Movement organized (alongside Leipzig's commemoration of the hundredth birthday of the "Battle of the Nations") a great meeting at Hohen Meissner, close to Kassel. Several thousand young "Wandervogel" discussed the problems of the movement, which was pacifist, nationalist, and populist in orientation. On the eve of the First World War, the *Jugendbewegung* counted approximately 25,000 members. After 1918, the movement could not regain its old cohesion, but its influence remained undeniable.

On the Wandervogel, see especially Hans Blüher, *Wandervogel. Geschichte einer Jugendbewegung* (*Birds of Passage: History of a Youth Movement*), 2 vols. (Berlin-Tempelhof: Bernhard Weise, 1912–1913); Fr. W. Foerster, *Jugendseele, Jugendbewegung, Jugendziel* (*Youth Soul, Youth Movement, Youth Goal*) (München-Leipzig: Rotapfel, 1923); Theo Herrle, *Die deutsche Jugendbewegung in ihren kulturellen Zusammenhängen* (*The German Youth Movement in its Cultural Context*) (Gotha-Stuttgart: Friedrich Andreas Perthes, 1924); Heinrich Ahrens, *Die deutsche Wandervogelbewegung von den Anfängen bis zum Weltkrieg* (*The German Birds of Passage Movement from its Origin to the World*

em, "Unser Leben," in their local journal. In 1913, at the age of 18, he left home. His travels ended in Verdun, where he joined the French Foreign Legion. A few months later, after a brief sojourn in Algeria where his training began at Siddi bel Abbes, his father was able to persuade him to return to Germany. Jünger resumed his studies at the Hanover Guild Institute, where he became familiar with the works of Nietzsche.

The First World War broke out on August 1st, 1914. Jünger volunteered on the first day. Assigned to the 73rd regiment of fusiliers, he received his marching orders on October 6th. On December 27th, he left for the front in Champagne. Jünger fought at Dorfes-les-Epargnes, at Douchy, at Moncy. He became squad leader in August 1915, sub-lieutenant in November, and from April 1916 underwent officer training at Croisilles. Two months later, he took part in the engagements on the Somme, where he was twice wounded. Upon his return to the front in November, with the rank of lieutenant, Jünger was wounded again near Saint-Pierre-Vaast. On December 16th he received the Iron Cross First Class. In February 1917, he became *Stosstruppführer* (leader of an assault battalion).

War) (Hamburg: Hansischer Gildenverlag, 1939); Werner Kindt, ed., *Grundschriften der deutschen Jugendbewegung* (*Fundamental Writings of the German Youth Movement*) (Dusseldorf-Köln: Eugen Diederichs, 1963); Bernhard Schneider, *Daten zur Geschichte der Jugendbewegung* (*Data on the History of the Youth Movement*) (Bad Godesberg: Voggenreiter, 1965); Walter Laqueur, *Die deutsche Jugendbewegung. Eine historische Studie* (*The German Youth Movement: A Historical Study*) (Köln: Wissenschaft und Politik, 1978); Otto Neuloh and Wilhelm Zilius, *Die Wandervogel. Eine empirisch-soziologische Untersuchung der frühen deutschen Jugendbewegung* (*The Birds of Passage: An Empirical Sociological Investigation of the Early German Youth Movement*) (Göttingen: Vandenhoeck und Ruprecht, 1982).

This was when the war bogged down while the human costs became terrifyingly immense. The French prepared Nivelle's bloody and useless offensive on the Chemin des Dames. At the head of his men, Jünger fought hand to hand in the trenches. Endless engagement, new wounds: in July on the front in Flanders, and also in December. Jünger was decorated with the Knight's Cross of the Order of the Hohenzollerns. During the offense of March 1918, he again led assault troops and was wounded. In August, another wound, this time near Cambrai. He ended the war in a military hospital, having been wounded fourteen times. That earned him the cross *Pour le merite*, the highest award in the German army. Only twelve subaltern officers of the ground forces (one of them the future Field Marshal Rommel) received this decoration during the whole First World War.

"ONE LIVED ONLY FOR THE IDEA"

Between 1918 and 1923, in the barracks at Hanover, Jünger began to write his first books, inspired by his experiences at the front. *Storm of Steel* (*In Stahlgewittern*), first published in 1919 by the author and in a new edition in 1922, was an immediate success. There followed *Battle as Inner Experience* (*Der Kampf als inneres Erlebnis*, 1922), *Copse 125* (*Das Wäldchen 125*, 1924), and *Fire and Blood* (*Feur und Blut*, 1925). Very quickly, Jünger was recognized as one of the most brilliant writers of his generation, even though, as Henri Plard points out, he first became known primarily as a specialist in military problems thanks to articles on modern warfare published in *Militär-Wochenblatt*.[5]

However, Jünger did not feel at home in a peacetime army. It no longer offered the adventure of the *Freikorps*. In 1923 he left the Reichswehr and entered Leipzig Univer-

---

[5] Henri Plard, "The Career of Ernst Jünger, 1920–1929," *Germanic Studies*, April–June 1978.

sity to study biology, zoology, and philosophy. On August 3rd, 1925, he married nineteen-year-old Gretha von Jeinsen. She gave him two children: Ernst in 1926 and Alexander in 1934.

At the same time, his political ideas matured thanks to the veritable cauldron of agitation among the factions of German public opinion: the disastrous Treaty of Versailles, which the Weimar Republic had accepted without disputing any of its clauses, was everywhere felt to be an unbearable *Diktat*. In the space of a few months Jünger had become one of the principal representatives of the national-revolutionary milieux, an important group of the Conservative Revolution that extended to the "Left" with the National Bolshevik movement rallying primarily around Ernst Niekisch.

Jünger's political writings appeared during the central period of the Republic (the "Stresemann era"), a provisional period of respite and apparent calm that ended in 1929. He would say later: "One lived only for the Idea."[6]

Initially, his ideas were expressed in journals. In September 1925, a former *Freikorps* leader, Helmut Franke, who had just published a book entitled *State within the State*,[7] launched the journal *Die Standarte*, which set out to "contribute towards a spiritual deepening of the thought of the Front." Jünger was on the editorial board, along with another representative of "soldatic nationalism," the writer Franz Schauwecker, born in 1890. Initially published as a supplement of the weekly magazine *Der Stahlhelm* (the organ of the association of war veterans also called Stahl-

---

[6] *Paris Journal*, vol. 2, April 20th, 1943. Jünger's journals have been published as *Strahlungen* (*Radiations*), vols. I–VI (Stuttgart: Klett-Cotta, 2015). Parts of the first two volumes appear in English as Ernst Jünger, *A German Officer in Occupied Paris: The War Journals: 1941–1945*, trans. Thomas S. Hansen and Abby J. Hansen (New York: Columbia University Press, 2019).

[7] Helmut Franke, *Staat im Staate* (Berlin: Stahlhelm, 1924).

helm)[8] and directed by Wilhelm Kleinau, *Die Standarte* had a considerable circulation: approximately 170,000 readers. Between September 1925 and March 1926, Jünger published nineteen articles there. Helmut Franke signed his contributions with the pseudonym "Gracchus." The whole anti-revolutionary young Right published there: Werner Beumelburg, Franz Schauwecker, Hans Henning von Grote, Friedrich Wilhelm Heinz, Goetz Otto Stoffregen, etc.

In *Die Standarte* Jünger immediately adopted a quite radical tone, very different from that of most Stahlhelm members. In an article published in October 1925, he criti-

---

[8] The Stalhelm association had been founded at the end of 1918 by Franz Seldte, born in Magdeburg in 1882, in reaction to the November revolution. His orientation to the Right was intensified the moment the Treaty of Versailles was signed in June of 1919. After the assassination of Walther Rathenau, in 1922, Stahlhelm was dissolved in Prussia, but the ban was lifted the following year. In 1925, it had around 260,000 members. In 1933, Seldte was named Minister of Labor in Hitler's first cabinet. The National Socialist regime went on to force Stahlhelm's integration into the Nationalsozialistischer Deutscher Frontkampferbund (NSDFB). Theodor Duesterberg, Seldte's assistant since 1924, who had immediately abandoned his functions, was arrested and imprisoned in June 1934. In 1935, the "liquidation" of Stahlhelm was complete. See on this subject: Wilhelm Kleinau, *Soldaten der Nation. Die geschichtliche Sendung des Stahlhelm* (*Soldiers of the Nation: The Historical Mission of the Stahlhelm*) (Berlin: Stahlhelm, 1933); Franz Seldte, ed., *Der NSDFB (Stahlhelm). Geschichte, Wesen und Aufgabe des Frontsoldatenbundes* (*The NSDFB (Stahlhelm): History, Essence, and Effect of the Frontline Soldiers Association*) (Berlin: Freiheitsverlag, 1935); Theodor Duesterberg, *Der Stahlhelm und Hitler* (*The Stahlhelm and Hitler*) (Wolfenbüttel-Hanover: Wolfenbütteler Verlagsanstalt, 1949); and Volker R. Berghahn, *Der Stahlhelm-Bund der Frontsoldaten* (*The Stahlhelm Association of Frontline Soldiers*) (Düsseldorf: Droste, 1966).

cised the theory of the "stab in the back" (*Dolchstoss*), which was accepted by almost all nationalists, namely that the German army was not defeated at the front but by a "stab in the back" at home. Jünger also emphasized that certain revolutionaries of the far Left had fought with distinction in the war.[9] Remarks of this kind caused a violent uproar. Quickly, the leaders of Stahlhelm moved to distance themselves from the young writer who had agitated their side.

In March 1926 *Die Standarte* was closed. But it was revived a month later under the abridged name *Standarte* with Jünger, Schauwecker, Kleinau, and Franke as co-editors. At this time, the ties with Stahlhelm were not entirely severed: the old soldiers continued to indirectly finance *Standarte*. Jünger and his friends reaffirmed their revolutionary calling. On June 3rd, 1926, Jünger published an appeal to all former front soldiers to unite for the creation of a "nationalist workers' republic," a motion that found no second.[10]

In August, at the urging of Otto Hörsing, co-founder of the *Reichsbanner Schwarz-Rot-Gold*, the ruling Social Democrats' security force, using the pretext of an article about Rathenau, banned *Standarte* for five months. On this pretext, Franz Seldte "decommissioned" its chief editor, Helmut Franke. Jünger quit in solidarity, and in November the two became, along with Wilhelm Weiss, the editors of another journal, *Arminius*. (*Standarte*, under

---

[9] Ernst Jünger, "Die Revolution," *Die Standarte*, 1, October 18, 1925.

[10] Cf. Louis Dupeux, *Strategie communiste et dynamique conservatrice. Essai sur les differents sens de l'expression «national-bolchevisme» en Allemagne, sous la Republique de Weimar, 1919–1933* (*Communist Strategy and Conservative Dynamics: Essay on the Different Meanings of the Expression "National-Bolshevism" in Germany under the Weimar Republic, 1919–1933*) (Paris: Honore Champion, 1976), p. 313.

different editorship, continued until 1929.)

In 1927, Jünger left Leipzig for Berlin, where he formed close ties with former *Freikorps* members and with the young *"bündisch"* movement. The latter, oscillating between military discipline and a very firm *esprit de corps*, tried to reconcile the adventurous romanticism of the Wandervogel with a more hierarchical, communitarian mode of organization. In particular, Jünger was closely connected to Werner Lass, born in Berlin in 1902, who in 1924 had been the founder, along with the old leader of the Rossbach *Freikorps* unit, of the Schilljugend (a youth movement named for Major Schill, who was killed during the struggle for liberation against Napoleon's occupation). In 1927, Lass left Rossbach and launched Freischar Schill, a *bündisch* group of which Jünger rapidly became the mentor (*Schirmherr*). From October 1927 to March 1928, Lass and Jünger collaborated to publish the journal *Der Vormarsch*, founded in June 1927 by another famous *Freikorps* leader, captain Ehrhardt.

"LOSING THE WAR TO WIN THE NATION"

During this time Jünger had a number of literary and philosophical influences. During the war, the experience of the front enabled him to resolve the triple influence of such late nineteenth-century French writers as Huysmans and Léon Bloy, of a kind of expressionism that still shows up clearly in *Battle as Inner Experience* (and especially in the first version of *The Adventurous Heart*), and of a kind of Baudelairian dandyism clearly present in *Storm* (*Sturm*), an early novel recently published.[11]

Armin Mohler likens the young Jünger to the Maurice

---

[11] Cf. Henri Plard, "Une oeuvre retrouvée d'Ernst Jünger: *Sturm* (1923)" ("A Rediscovered Work by Ernst Jünger: *Storm* [1923]), *Etudes germaniques,* October–December 1968, pp. 600–15. (Ernst Jünger, *Sturm* [Stuttgart: Ernst Klett, 1978]—Ed.)

Barrès of *Roman de l'Energie nationale* (*Novel of the National Energy*).[12] For the author of *Battle as Inner Experience*, as for the author of *Scènes et doctrines du nationalism* (*Scenes and Doctrines of Nationalism*),[13] nationalism is a substitute religion, a mode of enlarging and strengthening the soul, that results above all from a *deliberate choice*. The *decisionist* aspect of this orientation arises from the collapse of standards after the advent of the First World War.

The influence of Spengler and Nietzsche is also evident. In 1929, in an interview given to an English journalist, Jünger defined himself as a "disciple of Nietzsche," stressing that Nietzsche was the first to challenge the fiction of an abstract universal man, "sundering" this fiction into two concrete, diametrically opposed types: the strong and the weak. In 1922 Jünger passionately read the first volume of *The Decline of the West*, then the second volume as soon as it was released in December of the same year, when he wrote *Sturm*.

However, as we shall see, Jünger was no passive disciple. He was far from following Nietzsche and Spengler in the totality of their positions. The decline of the West in his eyes was not an inescapable fate; there were other alternatives than simply acquiescing to the reign of "Caesars." In the same way, if Jünger adopts Nietzsche's *questioning*, it was first and foremost to bring it to an end.

Ultimately, the war was the strongest influence, and Jünger initially drew the lesson of *agonism* from it. War must cause passion, but not hatred: the soldier on the

---

[12] Maurice Barrès, *Roman de l'Energie nationale*, was published in three volumes: *Les Déracinés* (*The Rootless*) (Paris: Bibliothèque Charpentier, 1897), *L'Appel au soldat* (*The Call to the Soldier*) (Paris: Librairie Plon, 1900), and *Leurs figures* (*Their Figures*) (Paris: Nelson, 1902).

[13] *Scènes et doctrines du nationalism* (Paris: Félix Juven, 1902).

other side of the trenches is not an incarnation of evil, but a simple figure of momentary adversity. It is because there is no absolute enemy (*Feind*), but only an adversary (*Gegner*), that "combat is always something holy." Another lesson is that life is nourished by death and vice-versa: "The most precious knowledge that one acquired from the school of the war," Jünger would write, "is that life, in its most secret heart, is indestructible."[14]

Granted, the war had been lost. But in virtue of the principle of the equivalence of contraries, this defeat also demanded a positive analysis. First, defeat or victory is not the most important issue of the war. Fundamentally activistic, the national revolutionist ideology professes a certain contempt of *goals*. One does not fight to attain victory; one fights to make war. Moreover, Jünger claimed, "the war is less a war between nations, than a war between different kinds of men. In all the nations that took part in that war, there are both victors and vanquished" (*Battle as Inner Experience*).

Better yet, defeat can become the means to victory. Indeed, it represents the very *condition* of this victory. As the epigraph of his book *Aufbruch der Nation* (*Awakening of the Nation*),[15] Franz Schauwecker used this stunning phrase: "It was necessary for us to lose the war to win the nation." Perhaps remembering the words of Léon Bloy, "All that happens is worthy," Jünger also says: "Germany was vanquished, but this defeat was salutary because it contributed to the destruction of the old Germany. . . . It was necessary to lose the war to win the nation."

Defeated by the Allied coalition, Germany will be able to return to herself and change in a revolutionary way. The defeat must be accepted as a means of *transmutation:*

---

[14] *Das Reich*, I, October 1, 1930, p. 3.
[15] Franz Schauwecker, *Aufbruch der Nation* (Berlin: Frundsberg, 1930).

in a quasi-alchemical way, the experience of the front must be "transmuted" into a new experience of the life of the nation. Such is the base of "soldierly nationalism."

It was in the war, Jünger continues, that German youth acquired "the assurance that the old paths no longer lead anywhere, and that it is necessary to blaze new ones." An irreversible rupture (*Umbruch*), the war abolished all old values. Any reactionary attitude, any desire to regress, became impossible. The energy that had been unleashed in the fight for the fatherland, can from now on serve the fatherland in a new form. The war, in other words, furnished the *model for the peace*. In *The Worker*, one reads: "The battle front and the Labor front are identical" (p. 109).

The central idea is that the war, as superficially meaningless as it may appear, actually has a deep meaning. This cannot be grasped by rational investigation but only by feeling *(Ahnen)*. The positive interpretation that Jünger gives war is not, contrary to what is too often asserted, primarily dependent on the exaltation of "warrior values." It proceeded from a political concern to find a *purpose* in light of which the sacrifice of the dead soldiers could no longer be considered "useless."

From 1926 onwards, Jünger called tirelessly for the formation of a united front of nationalist groups and movements. At the same time, he sought—without notable success—to change them. For Jünger too, nationalism must be alchemically "transmuted." It must be freed of any sentimental attachment to the old Right and become *revolutionary*. It must take note of the decline of the bourgeois world apparent in the novels of Thomas Mann (*Buddenbrooks*) or Alfred Kubin (*Die andere Seite*).

From this point of view, what is essential is the fight against liberalism. In *Arminius* and *Der Vormarsch*, Jünger attacks the liberal order symbolized by the literati, the humanistic intellectuals who support an "anemic" society, the cynical internationalists whom Spengler sees as the true authors of the November Revolution and who claimed that the millions who perished in the Great War died for nothing.

At the same time, he stigmatizes the "bourgeois tradition" invoked by the nationalists and the members of the Stahlhelm, these *"petit bourgeois [Spiessbürger]* who, because of the war, slipped into a lion's skin."[16] Tirelessly, he took on the Wilhelmian spirit, the worship of the past, the taste of the pan-Germanists for "museology" (*musealer Betrieb*). In March 1926, he coined the term "neo-nationalism," which he opposed to "grandfather nationalism" (*Altvaternationalismus*).

Jünger defended Germany, but for him the nation is much more than a country. It is an *idea:* everywhere that this idea enflames the spirit is Germany. In April 1927, in *Arminius,* Jünger took an implicitly nominalist position: he states that he no longer believes in any general truths, any universal morals, any notion of "mankind" as a collective being everywhere sharing the same conscience and the same rights. "We believe," he says, "in the value of the particular" (*Wir glauben an den Wert des Besonderen*).

At a time when the traditional Right preached individualism against collectivism, when the *völkisch* groups were enthralled with the return to the earth and the mystique of "nature," Jünger exalted technology and condemned the individual. Born from bourgeois rationality, he explains in *Arminius,* all-powerful technology has now turned against those who engendered it. The more technological the world becomes, the more the individual disappears; neo-nationalism must be the first to embrace this truth. Moreover, it is in the great cities "that the nation will be won." For the national-revolutionists, "the city is a front."

---

[16] *Der Vormarsch,* December 1927.

Around Jünger a "Berlin group" soon formed, where representatives of various currents of the Conservative Revolution met: Franz Schauwecker and Helmut Franke; the writer Ernst von Solomon; the Nietzschean anti-Christian Friedrich Hielscher, editor of *Das Reich*; the neo-conservatives August Winnig (whom Jünger first met in the autumn of 1927 through the philosopher Alfred Baeumler) and Albrecht Erich Gunther, co-editor with Wilhelm Stapel of *Deutsches Volkstum*; the National Bolsheviks Ernst Niekisch and Karl O. Paetel; and of course Friedrich Georg Jünger, Ernst Jünger's younger brother, who was also a well-known thinker.

Friedrich Georg Jünger, whose own development is of great importance to that of his elder brother, was born in Hanover on September 1, 1898. His career closely paralleled his brother's. He too volunteered for the Great War; in 1916 he saw combat on the Somme and became the leader of his squad. In 1917 he was seriously wounded on the front in Flanders and spent several months in military hospitals. He returned to Hanover at the end of hostilities, and after a brief period as a lieutenant in the Reichswehr, he decided in 1920 to study law, defending his doctoral dissertation in 1924.

From 1926 on, Friedrich regularly contributed articles to the journals on which his brother collaborated: *Die Standarte, Arminius, Der Vormarsch,* etc. In the collection *Der Aufmarsch*, edited by Ernst Jünger, he also published a short essay entitled "Aufmarsch of Nationalismus" ("Deployment of Nationalism").[17] He was influenced by Nietzsche, Sorel, Klages, Stefan George, and Rilke, whom he frequently quoted and to whom he dedicated a volume of his own poetry.[18]

---

[17] *Der Aufmarsch*, foreword by Ernst Jünger (Berlin: Vormarsch, 1926; 2nd ed., Berlin: Vormarsch, 1928).

[18] The first study published on him was Franz Josef

In April 1928, Ernst Jünger entrusted the editorship of *Der Vormarsch* to his friend Friedrich Hielscher. Hielscher edited *Der Vormarsch* for a few months, after which the journal, published by Fritz Söhlmann, came under the control of the Jungdeutscher Orden (Jungdo) and took a completely different direction. Of Hielscher, to whom he was very attached (and whom he referred to as "Bodo" or "Bogo" in his notebooks), Jünger once said that he presented a curious "mixture of rationalism and naïveté."

Born on May 31st, 1902, in Guben, after the Great War Hielscher joined the *Freikorps*, then became involved in the *bündisch* movement, in particular the Freischar Schill of Werner Lass. In 1928, he published a doctoral thesis, *Die Selbstherrlichkeit (Self-Glory),*[19] in which he sought to define the foundations of a German Right based on Nietzsche, Spengler, and Max Weber. Moreover, Hielscher was, along with his friend Gerhard von Tevenar, passionate about "European social-regionalism" and sought to coordinate the actions of regionalist and separatist movements to create a "Europe of the fatherlands" on a federal model. Also influenced by the thought of Eriugena, Meister Eckhart, Luther, Shakespeare, and Goethe, he wrote a "political theology of the Empire" entitled *Das Reich (The Empire)*[20] and founded a small neopagan church that sometimes brought him closer to the *völkisch* movement.

Under the Third Reich, Hielscher played a leading role in the research of the Ahnenerbe, while he and his students maintained close contact with the "inner emigration." The Hitler regime reproached him in particular for

---

Schöningh, "Friedrich Georg Jünger und der preussische Stil" ("Friedrich Georg Jünger and the Prussian Style"), *Hochland,* February 1935, pp. 476–77.

[19] Friedrich Hielscher, *Die Selbstherrlichkeit* (Berlin: Vormarsch, 1928).

[20] Friedrich Hielscher, *Das Reich* (Berlin: Das Reich, 1931).

"philosemitism,"[21] ordering his arrest in September 1944. Thrown in prison, Hielscher escaped death only because of the intervention of Wolfram Sievers. After the war Hielscher retired to the Black Forest and published his autobiography, *Funfzig Jahre unter Deutschen* (*Fifty Years among Germans*),[22] but the majority of his writings (e.g., the "liturgy" of his neopagan church, a verse version of the *Niebulungenlied*, etc.) remain unpublished.[23]

A few months later, in January 1930, Jünger became co-editor with Werner Lass of *Die Kommenden* (*The Coming*), the weekly newspaper founded five years before by the writer Wilhelm Kotzde (who at the time had a great influence over the *bündisch* youth movement, particularly the tendency that had evolved toward National Bolshevism), along with Hans Ebeling and especially Karl O. Paetel, who simultaneously collaborated on *Die Kommenden,* as well as *Die sozialistische Nation* (*The Socialist Nation*) and *Antifaschistische Briefe* (*Anti-Fascist Letters*).

Regarded as one of the principal representatives, along with Niekisch, of German National Bolshevism, Karl O. Paetel was born in Berlin on November 23rd, 1906. *Bündisch*, then national revolutionary, he adopted National Bolshevism about 1930. From 1928 to 1930 he edited the monthly magazine *Das junge Volk* (*The Young People*). From 1931 to 1933 he published the journal *Die sozialistische Nation* (*The Socialist Nation*).

Imprisoned several times after Hitler's rise to power, in 1935 Paetel emigrated to Prague, then Scandinavia. In 1939, he was stripped of his German nationality and con-

---

[21] Cf. *Das Reich,* p. 332.

[22] Friedrich Hielscher, *Funfzig Jahre unter Deutschen* (Hamburg: Rowohlt, 1954).

[23] On his role in resistance against Hitler, see Rolf Kluth, "Die Widerstandgruppe Hielscher" ("The Hielscher Resistance Group"), *Puis,* December 7, 1980, pp. 22–27.

demned to death *in absentia*. Interned in French concentration camps between January and June 1940, he escaped, reached Portugal, and finally settled in New York in January 1941.

In the United States, beginning in 1946, Paetel published the newspaper *Deutsche Blatter* (*German Pages*). The same year, with Carl Zuckmayer and Dorothy Thompson, he published a collection of documents on "internal emigration."[24] He also devoted several essays to Jünger.[25] After having launched a new newspaper, *Deutsche Gegenwart* (*German Present*) (1947–1948), Paetel returned to Germany in 1949 and continued to publish a great number of works. Decorated in 1968 with the *Bundesverdienstkreuz* (Federal Service Cross), he died on May 4th, 1975.[26]

---

[24] Karl O. Paetel, *Deutsche innere Emigration. Dokumente und Beitrage. Antinationalsozialistische Zeugnisse aus Deutschland* (*German Internal Emigration: Documents and Contributions. Anti-National Socialist Testimonies from Germany*) (New York: Friedrich Krause, 1946).

[25] Karl O. Paetel, *Ernst Jünger. Die Wandlung eines deutschen Dichters und Patrioten* (*Ernst Jünger: The Transformation of a German Poet and Patriot*) (New York: Friedrich Krause, 1946); *Ernst Jünger. Weg und Wirkung. Eine Einfuhrung* (*Ernst Jünger: Way and Influence. An Introduction*) (Stuttgart: Ernst Klett, 1949); *Ernst Jünger. Eine Bibliographie* (*Ernst Jünger: A Bibliography*) (Stuttgart: Lutz and Meyer, 1953); *Ernst Jünger in Selbstzeugnissen und Bilddokumenten* (*Ernst Jünger in His Own Words and Pictures*) (Reinbek near Hamburg: Rowohlt, 1962).

[26] Karl O. Paetel's personal papers are today partly in the archives of the *Jugendbewegung* (Burg Ludwigstein, Witzenhausen) and in part in the Karl O. Paetel Collection of the State University of New York, Albany. On Paetel, see his history of National Bolshevism: *Versuchung oder Chance? Zur Geschichte des deutschen Nationalbolschewismus* (*Temptation or Opportunity? Toward a History of German National Bolshevism*) (Göttingen: Musterschmid, 1965) and his posthumous autobiography, published by Wolfgang D. Elfe and John M. Spalek: *Reise*

Jünger also collaborated on the journal *Widerstand* (*Resistance*) founded and edited by Niekisch beginning in July 1926. The two men met in the autumn of 1927, and the two quickly became good friends. Jünger wrote: "If one wants to put the program that Niekisch developed in *Widerstand* in terms of stark alternatives, it would be something like this: against the bourgeois and for the Worker, against the Western world and for the East." Indeed, National Bolshevism, which has multiple tendencies and varieties, joins the idea of class struggle to a communitarian, if not collectivist, idea of the nation. "Collectivization," affirms Niekisch, "is the social form that the organic will must adopt if it is to affirm itself in the face of the fatal effects of technology."[27] According to Niekisch, in the final analysis the national movement and the communist movement have the same adversary, as the fight against the occupation of the Ruhr appeared to demonstrate, and this is why the two "proletarian nations" of Germany and Russia must strive for an understanding. "The liberal democratic parliamentarian flees from decision," declared Niekisch. "He does not want to fight, but to talk. . . . The Communist wants a decision. . . . In his roughness, there is something of the hardness of the military camp; in him there is more Prussian hardness than he knows, even more than in a Prussian bourgeois."[28] These ideas influenced a considerable portion of the national revolutionary movement. Jünger himself, as seen by Louis Dupeux, was "fascinated by the problems of Bolshevism"—but was never a National Bolshevik in the strict sense.

---

ohne Urzeit. Autobiography (*Journey without Beginning: Autobiography*) (London: World of Books and Worms: Georg Heintz, 1982).

[27] "Menschenfressende Technik" ("Man-Eating Technology"), *Widerstand*, 4, 1931.

[28] "Entscheidung" ("Decision"), *Widerstand*, 1930, p. 134.

In July of 1931, Werner Lass and Jünger withdrew from *Die Kommenden*. In September, Lass founded the journal *Der Umsturz* (*Overthrow*), which he made the organ of the Freischar Schill and which, until its disappearance in February 1933, openly promoted National Bolshevism. But Jünger was in a very different frame of mind. In the space of a few years, using a whole series of journals as so many walls for sticking up posters, he traversed the whole field of his properly *political* evolution. It was, as he would write, a milk train "that one gets on and gets off along the way." The watchwords he had formulated did not have the success that he hoped for; his calls for unity were not heard. For some time, Jünger felt estranged from all political currents. He had no more sympathy for the rising National Socialism than for the traditional national leagues. All the national movements, he explained in an article in *Suddeutsche Monatshefte* (*South German Monthly*),[29] be they traditionalist, legitimist, economist, reactionary, or National Socialist, draw their inspiration from the past, and, in this respect, are "liberal" and "bourgeois." Divided between the neoconservatives and the National Bolsheviks, the national revolutionary groups no longer commanded respect. In fact, Jünger no longer believed in the possibility of collective action. (In the first version of *The Adventurous Heart*, he wrote: "Today one can no longer make collective efforts for Germany."[30]) As Niekisch was to emphasize in his autobiography, Jünger intended to trace a more personal and *interior* way of dealing with the current situation.[31] "Jünger, this perfect Prussian officer

---

[29] *Suddeutsche Monatshefte*, September 1930, pp. 843–45.

[30] Ernst Jünger, *Das Abenteuerliche Herz: Aufzeichnungen bei Tag und Nacht* (*The Adventurous Heart: Sketches by Day and Night*) (Berlin: Frundsberg, 1929), p. 153.

[31] *Erinerrungen eines deutschen Revolutionärs* (*Memories of a German Revolutionary*), *Wissenschaft u. Politik*, vol. I, 1974, p. 191.

who subjects himself to the hardest discipline," wrote Marcel Decombis, "would never again be able to fit in a collectivity."[32] His brother, who had abandoned his legal career in 1928, evolved in the same direction. He wrote about Greek poetry, the American novel, Kant, and Dostoyevsky. The two brothers undertook a series of voyages: Sicily (1929), the Balearic Islands (1931), Dalmatia (1932), and the Aegean Sea.

Ernst and Friedrich Georg Jünger continued, of course, to publish some articles, particularly in *Widerstand*. In total, Ernst Jünger published eleven articles in *Standarte*, twenty-eight in *Arminius*, twelve in *Der Vormarsch*, and eighteen in *Widerstand*. Like his brother, he collaborated on *Widerstand* until its prohibition in December 1934. But the properly journalistic period of their engagement was over. Between 1929 and 1932, Ernst Jünger concentrated all his efforts on new books, starting with the first version of *The Adventurous Heart* (1929), then the essay "Die totale Mobilmachung," ("Total Mobilization," 1931), and finally *Der Arbeiter. Herrschaft und Gestalt* (*The Worker: Dominion and Form*), published in 1932 in Hamburg by the Hanseatische Verlagsanstalt of Benno Ziegler and reprinted many times before 1945.

II.

The first part of *The Worker* revolves around a fundamental notion that Jünger chooses to express with the word *Gestalt*, literally "form," but more accurately "figure." It is not an easy notion to define.[33] It must be seen as a

---

[32] Marcel Decombis, *Ernst Jünger* (Paris: Aubier, 1943).

[33] Jünger himself clearly perceived the limitation inherent in the words and concepts to which he had recourse. "All these concepts (figure, type, organic construction, total)," he writes, "are *there—nota bene*—as concepts to be conceived. We do not insist on them. They can just as well be forgotten or banished,

totality, a globality, but also as a meaningful type. Already in his books on the war, Jünger had displayed a predilection for the enumeration and analysis of "types."[34] Reacting to dissociative, analytical reason, Jünger specifies that the figure is significant only insofar as it constitutes a whole endowed with properties not found in any of its elements. The figure, he says, is "a whole that is greater than the sum of its parts" (*ein Ganzes das mehr als die Summe seiner Teile umfasst*). We see immediately the analogy with the "anti-reductionist" principle systematized by the Gestalt psychology of Wolfgang Köhler. But we are not here faced with a psychological concept. The Jüngerian Gestalt is an "organic concept" (*organischer Begriff*) directly associated with the world and life. As such, it is opposed to the *idea*, in the sense of the *perception* of the representation of a subject. The notion of figure, Jünger holds, is more closely related to Leibniz's monad than to Plato's idea, closer to Goethe's ur-plant (*Urpflanze*) than to Hegel's synthesis.[35]

The figure is a type, but it is also, and even more, a *power constructive of types* which incarnates the dominant spirit of a given epoch, thus giving the world its principal meaning. The figure, in effect, is a source of *meaning*. "By figure," writes, Jünger, "we refer to a superior reality that

---

since they have only been used as working tools for grasping a determinate reality that subsists beyond all concepts and in spite of all concepts; the reader's task is to see through the description as through an optical system" (p. 296).

[34] A rapprochement has already been carried out between *Gestalt* and the Jungian archetype, especially as regards dreams and types, by Volker Katzmann in his book on Jünger's "magic realism": *Ernst Jüngers magischer Realismus* (*Ernst Jünger's Magical Realism*) (Hildesheim: Georg Olms, 1975), p. 54. Note also that Jünger was, along with Mircea Eliade, one of the founders of the journal *Antaios*.

[35] Letter to Henri Plard, September 24, 1978.

gives a meaning to phenomena." This question of meaning is essential. Meaning, here, is something relative that has absolute value. The figure does not give a meaning in the classic sense of causality, but rather in the fashion of an *imprint*. It refers to a humanity that, in its turn, is (*qua subjectum*) at the basis of all being. If the epoch has a meaning, this is because it is *marked* as with a seal by a given figure. Heidegger, speaking to Jünger, will say: "The figure as well remains for you something only accessible in a *seeing*. It is the seeing that among the Greeks was called *idein*, a word Plato uses for a gaze which considers not the change of sense perception but the immutable, being, the idea, the *eidos* . . ." As a source of meaning—source of all "bestowal of meaning" and thus of all justification—the figure is an "acting magnitude" with a metaphysical value. It is a "preformed power" (*vorgeformte Macht*). It is that *destined* potential which only accedes to being by the will of the man who senses its "call." It depends only on man whether the figure is something other than what it is—"a figure is, and there is no evolution which can augment or diminish it"—but it depends on him whether it fully accedes to the state of an existing thing, whether it endows itself fully with the dimension of *depth*.

The figure can only be understood "dialectically," so much does it comprehend different aspects. One must get used to thinking of it as both unchanging and localized. Its relation to history, moreover, is complex. The figure is not so much the product of history as *that which permits history to take place*. While remaining unchangeable, it determines the *movement* of history:

> A historical figure is, in the most profound sense, independent of the time and circumstance of which it appears to be born. . . . History does not engender figures; on the contrary, it transforms itself with the figure.

History is thus related to a metaphysics of being. In *The Forest Path*, Jünger will say that our epoch is poor in great men but rich in figures.

Possessing the individual and dissolving him within itself, the figure "bears its own scale within itself." It is itself its own measure. From an epistemological point of view, it quite naturally orients toward a new determination of value. But this value—which, as we shall see, is bound up with the metaphysics of the Will to Power—cannot be appreciated according to current measures. The figure is situated beyond good and evil. Not only is it not subject to morality, it is only from the figure that a morality can be developed. The figure "is not subject to the court of the triple criteria of truth, beauty, and morality; it is the figure, on the contrary, who determines aesthetic, scientific, and moral norms"[36] The role of the theoretician is not therefore to pass any sort of judgment, moral or otherwise, upon the figure of an epoch, but rather to seek to identify it, to recognize it intuitively. "The essential point is not knowing whether something is good or bad, beautiful or ugly, true or false, but discovering what figure it belongs to." There is no universal value, morality, or ideal. Rather there are only historical figures identified and "heroically" assumed. The figure's awareness is related to its *realization*. Its perception, its *total* identification, is a "revolutionary act that restores to life all its plenitude and recognizes it as such."

What, then, is the dominant figure of our time? It is work, says Jünger—and consequently in the figure of the Worker the "type of the rising generation" resides. This work of which Jünger speaks is neither an activity revolving around economic production nor a "law of humanity." Nor is it the result of any original sin: it does not represent any form of "alienation"; it is not reducible to any profes-

---

[36] Marcel Decombris, *Ernst Jünger*, op. cit.

sional activity. It subsumes, rather, all creation aimed at
giving form to the world, all affirmation of power, all ex-
penditure of energy. Work is that through which the
modern world is *totally mobilized*. It is, says Jünger, "the
expression of a particular being [*der Ausdruck eines besonderen Seins*] that seeks to fill its space, its time, and its
laws." The dominant form of our epoch, it represents a
principle that has no negative counterpart. Being beyond
contraries, it surpasses and resolves all contradictions.
Nothing can exist today that is not conceived as work.

> The speed of the fist, the thought, the heart, life
> which goes on day and night, science, love, art,
> faith, worship, war: everything is work; work is also
> the vibration of atoms, the force that moves the
> stars and the solar systems.

In this sense, work is less activity itself than the will that is
at work in all activity, the *will to will* that, having become
work, passes from the domain of the elementary to that of
history.

Similarly, the idea that the essential quality of the
Worker[37] is economic in nature is, according to Jünger, a
"legend," a typical bourgeois product of thought: by defining the Worker as an economic agent, the bourgeoisie
merely expresses the "dictatorship" of its own mode of
thought. Jünger constantly insists that the Worker is *not*
an "economic figure."

> One must not understand by the term *Worker* either
> an estate in the ancient sense or a class in the sense
> of the revolutionary dialectic of the nineteenth cen-
> tury. . . . The Worker is not the representative of a

---

[37] The word *Arbeiter* has sometimes been rendered in French
by *Ouvrier*. This translation is obviously much too restrictive.
(Benoist employs *Travailleur*—Ed.)

new class, a new society, a new economy, because he is nothing if he is not more than all of that, viz., the representative of a particular figure acting according to its own laws, pursuing its own mission, and possessing a freedom of its own.

Just as work dominates all social milieus, the Worker does not identify himself with the proletariat—or else, if he does, he incarnates a new proletariat in which *all classes are subsumed*. To define the Worker, one must appeal to notions of an altogether different sort: a subterranean substance with hidden potentialities, a spirit in which "destiny and freedom meet on a knife's edge," a perception of the world at once cold and tragic, a "new humanity equal in value to all the great characters of history." The State of the *Worker* thus has nothing to do with the workers' state of which Marx speaks. To the *Arbeiterschaft*, the working class, Jünger opposes the *Arbeitertum*, which refers both to the state of belonging to and identifying with the essence of work, and to an organic community of all who participate in that essence.[38]

---

[38] The opposition between *Arbeitertum* and proletariat has also been developed by August Winnig, especially in *Der Glaube an das Proletariat* (*Faith in the Proletariat*) (Munich: Milavida, 1926) and *Vom Proletariat zum Arbeitertum* (*From Proletarian to Working Class*) (Hamburg: Hanseatische Verlagsanstalt, 1930), but with a more narrowly political resonance. Former Oberpräsident of East Prussia at the end of the First World War, Winnig (1878–1956) was excluded from the Social Democratic Party for his support of the Kapp Putsch. He affiliated himself with the neoconservatives about 1923, then with the National Bolsheviks, and was Niekisch's associate in editing *Widerstand* between July 1927 and 1930. Beginning in 1924 he was also Friedrich Hielscher's mentor, orienting him toward Jünger. His work seeks to take the class struggle away from Marxism, the proletariat away from the class struggle, and the Worker away

One should, however, distrust any narrowly anti-Marxist interpretation of the book, which Jünger himself warned against:

> I reject the anti-Marxist interpretation. Marx finds his place in the system of *The Worker*, but he does not fill it in its entirety. One can say the same thing concerning its attitude to Hegel. I presume, moreover, that Hegel would be better accommodated by the Worker as figure than by his reduction to the economic dimension, which only represents one of his aspects.[39]

Marxism, which Jünger said in *Die Kommenden* is useful because it is corrosive,[40] is *included* (and surpassed) in *The Worker*. What Jünger rejects, in fact, is the idea that historical becoming is determined, in the last analysis, by the economy. Work does not derive from the economy. It is not determined by costs, surplus value, or commercial interest; profit, while it can be one of work's consequences, cannot constitute its goal. Marx only grasped work in its historical and sociological form. Jünger perceived its metaphysical dimension and gave it a range extending "from the atom to the galaxies." Marx believed that the Worker

---

from the proletariat. The partisan of an "ethical socialism" based on the Prussian idea and the German sense of "service," he wrote: "The proletariat is more than a mere class. It is above all part of a people, i.e., part of a biological and historical unity the laws of whose life are also valid for the proletariat." In Winnig as in Jünger, though at different levels, we perceive the importance attached to *type*, notions that gather historical elements as well as sociological, psychological, or moral elements, and which a whole generation made quite a fuss about ("Prussian type" in Spengler, "hero and merchant" in Sombart, "hero and bourgeois" in Bogislav von Selchow, etc.).

[39] Letter to Henri Plard, op. cit.

[40] *Die Kommenden,* no. 13, March 28, 1930.

was going to transform into an "artist." Jünger saw how the artist was already transforming into a Worker.

The Worker is certainly susceptible of an economic definition, but this definition must be subordinated to power (*Macht*). It is, in fact, by power that the Worker manifests himself: the *representation* of the figure, writes Jünger, is the domination of the Worker as a "new and particular Will to Power" (p. 70). This domination (*Herrschaft*) is "only possible today as representation of the figure of the Worker" (p. 192). The Will to Power, in other words, expresses itself through work and as work in a world that it "mobilizes." The figure, Jünger would go on to say,

> represents the world spirit in a particular epoch, i.e., the dominant general spirit, including from the economic point of view. The fundamental problem is power; it determines the rest. This is perfectly verified today: everywhere where workers' parties are in power, from China by way of Russia all the way to East Germany, questions of power take precedence over economic questions. If one demonstrates to these states, and also to Western communists, that they are departing from Marx, the objection is well-founded, if somewhat stale. Behind the representation of the world spirit is matter, not pure idea. Although Hegel affirms otherwise, often radically, theory does not determine reality; on the contrary, it is reality that engenders ideas and that modifies itself on the basis of itself. Even technological discovery, which is neither accidental nor "invented," suffers constraint. Here is a conception of the matter that goes back to a stage earlier than Plato—it is not materialist, but material.[41]

---

[41] Letter to Henri Plard, op. cit.

At about the same time, he would declare:

> The economic is secondary for me. Whoever has power reigns over the economy, while the latter not only does not allow accession to power but has a weakening effect every time it is expressed in politics.[42]

Insofar as it manifests itself through power, the figure of the Worker is certainly a heroic figure. But it is above all, as Albrecht Erich Günther has already remarked, a *metaphysical* figure.[43] "The figure of the Worker," writes Jünger

> is recumbent and immobile within being, more deeply than all the orders and symbols through which it confirms itself, more deeply than constitutions and their works, than men and their communities, those things that are the changing traits of a figure whose fundamental character subsists in an untransformable way.

This can already be perceived in the vocabulary: the words employed in *The Worker* "are not even waves, but only a sparkling above the unfathomable depths of being." The Worker is not Nietzsche's Overman: relative to the figure, the latter is outmoded; it is becoming "paleontological."[44] Depositary of the *elemental*, the Worker is in fact a *titanic* character: "in my mind, he is a metaphysical character, the first of the titans to make his appearance in our time."[45]

---

[42] Interview with Jean Louis de Rambures, *Le Monde*, June 20, 1978.

[43] *Deutsches Volkstum*, January 1933.

[44] Letter to Walter Patt, August 4, 1980.

[45] Interview with Jean-Louis de Rambures, op. cit.

The figure antithetical to that of the Worker can obviously only be the *bourgeois*. In Jünger, as we have seen, anti-liberalism is above all an anti-bourgeoisism whose bases are not only political but also spiritual and ethical. At the time of *Arminius* and *Der Vormarsch*, Jünger vigorously denounced the liberal philosophy, which only accords abstract rights to individuals artificially considered as being in themselves, reproaching it with the charge that it is foreign to the German spirit, and even to spirit *per se*. It is *sincerity* in the struggle against bourgeoisism, he said, that permits recognition of the true national spirit and true socialism. In *The Worker* this critique is taken up again, but it is carried to a whole different level.

Of course, the bourgeois no more defines himself principally as the representative of a social class than does the Worker. He is, rather, a *type* who serves as the vehicle for a way of life and thought, a scale of values, a state of mind that one finds in all social categories, including that of the "proletariat" whose sole ambition is to ascend to the bourgeois economic class. So, the critique Jünger makes of the bourgeois is totally different from that of Marx. To the bourgeois, Jünger *denies all metaphysical value*. The bourgeois, in contrast to the Worker, only reasons in a *utilitarian* manner. He wants to receive as much as possible from life and give back as little as possible. Above all, he values *security*. For centuries, he has enclosed himself within fortified castles and large cities. Consequently, he has naturally seen great cities as "ideal centers of security" (*Hochburgen der Sicherheit*). Moved by fear and envy, seeking profit and leisure, he continues to this day to barricade himself against life. Given his level of being, he is incapable of conceiving a *historic* action, of realizing decisive, energetic actions. He always keeps his distance from the "elementals" from which the Worker derives his power. These powers of the elemental, whether of strife, love, nature, or death, he considers "unreasonable" or "immoral."

Society, for the bourgeois, is the result of a voluntary, rational act, of a contract resting on the security of the principle of equality for all. (This is also why, in the case of an international conflict, he is so concerned to know who is "wrong" and who is "right.") In short, the Worker and the bourgeois differ as dawn does from dusk.

The advent of the figure of the Worker is bound up with a new state of society, to which Jünger gives the name "total mobilization" (*totale Mobilmachung*). This expression is explained at length in an essay published under the same title, which constitutes a sort of "preface" to *The Worker* and exhibits a deepening of reflection on the subject of war begun during the previous period.[46]

It is, in fact, the evolution of military technology that most clearly marks the entry into the era of total mobilization. From the days when Clausewitz had been the first to evoke the idea of "absolute war," the conditions of warfare had greatly evolved. In Germany at the beginning of the century, infantry was recognized as the principal branch: "It alone overcomes the last resistance. It bears the principal burden of combat and makes the greatest sacrifices. That is also why it achieves the most glory" (infantry regulations of 1906). By confirming the decline of cavalry and the disappearance of the autonomous artillery duel, the First World War appeared to confirm the idea that the infantry decides the outcome of battle, and that all other branches should be considered subordinate. At the same

---

[46] *Total Mobilization* first appeared in 1930 as part of a collective work: Ernst Jünger, ed., *Krieg und Krieger* (*War and Warrior*) (Berlin: Junker und Dünnhaupt, 1930), pp. 9–30, before being published separately the following year: *Die Totale Mobilmachung* (Berlin: Verlag für Zeitkritik, 1931). A French translation exists: *La mobilisation totale*, in Lion Murard and Patrick Zylberman, eds., *Le Soldat du travail: guerre, fascisme, et Taylorisme* (*The Soldier of Labor: War, Fascism, and Taylorism*) (Paris: Recherches, 1978), pp. 35–53.

time, the machine gun became the offensive and defensive weapon *par excellence*. The "assault platoons" or commando squads, to which Jünger belonged, then constituted a particular category of infantry specially trained for offensive action within the framework of the *war of position* (which was the great historical innovation of the war of 1914–18). "Resolute attack" and "all for all" were the watchwords for these small task forces: "attack consists in carrying fire to the enemy, at the closest possible distance if the situation demands. Victory is sealed by knife attacks." Finally, we see the air force, trench guns, and gas.

Particularly beginning in 1916, the "genius of war" and the "spirit of progress" concluded a close alliance expressed above all in the increasingly marked primacy of the *technical* element and the setting in motion of increasingly momentous quantities of energy. This development made the First World War fundamentally different from all previous conflicts. It marked the end of "chivalry," the end of the era of traditional heroic values. In the trenches, Jünger saw classic battle evolve into a *Materialschlacht*, a "material battle." Henceforth the function of troops was relegated to that of "materiel"; war is "totally impregnated with the spirit that created the machines." At the same time, martial exaltation changed into a routine symbolized by *position*. "The trenches made war into a trade, the soldiers into workmen of death, polished and repolished by a bloody routine," wrote Jünger already in *War, Our Mother*. And in *Copse 125*, observing the importance assumed by the "*technically* instructed assault leaders," he remarks:

> The toughest sons of war, the men who march at the head of their troops, those who drive the assault tanks, the planes, the submarines, are all amazing *technicians*; and it is through them that the modern State represents itself in combat.

At this point the question arises: in such a context does the death of a soldier still have any significance at all? The response lies in total mobilization. As war becomes a technical enterprise, traditional distinctions are effaced: between combatant and non-combatant, military and civilian, the front lines and the rear, and even, finally, between a state of belligerence and a state of non-belligerence. There are no longer war and peace, but a permanent global fight that mobilizes all men without distinction. This process of mobilization, born of technology, surpasses it. It is spiritual and "ideological." A disposition (*Bereitschaft*) to mobilization appears everywhere; it even reaches pacifists! "The technical side of total mobilization," writes Jünger, "is not its decisive aspect. Its principle, like the presupposition of all technology, is buried deeper: we define it as the *disposition* to be mobilized." Increasingly, the *capacity for mobilization* reveals itself as a key factor in the destiny of peoples. Moreover, the transformation of war very quickly entailed a transformation of society. By putting an end to the role of the individual fighter, war has made soldiers mere parts of a whole, of a collectivity globally oriented toward fighting, and has thereby revealed this fight as an *aspect of work*. "The image of war, which represents it as an armed action," emphasizes Jünger,

> increasingly fades, making way for a much broader representation that conceives it as a giant process of work. . . . Total mobilization changes the landscape, but not the meaning, when instead of armies, it sets masses in motion and unleashes a process of civil war.

Such a "work process" transforms the universe into a "landscape/construction site," into a true "Vulcan's forge." The world is henceforward both *mobile* and *mobilized*.

The *meaning* that the battlefield seems to have lost was in fact now found everywhere at a higher level. So, the sacrifice of men is not meaningless; such is the meaning of the death of soldiers.

If the Great War, due to the "radical requisitioning" it occasioned, must be regarded as "a historical event that surpasses in importance the French Revolution," this is because it gave birth to a new man. The Great War produced the type of the "*forge-tempered* man," and with him appeared a new mode of action. With total mobilization the figures of the Worker and the Soldier blended together: "The war front and the work front are identical." The Soldier has become a Worker, the Worker has become a Soldier. More precisely, the figure of the soldier, born of work, of technological development, has in his turn given form to the figure of the Worker, which conserves its essential traits but gives them a more general scope.[47]

With the First World War also commences the time of the collective "we" (*Wirzeit*), by way of opposition to that of the individual "I" (*Ichzeit*). It is clear that for Jünger the age of the individual is over. Moreover, he enumerates the traits of society that are so many factors of uniformization: the decline of the rural world, the development of highway networks, the appearance of collective leisure activities, the evolution of parties, the retreat of theater in favor of film, of the stage before the speaker's tribune, of the

---

[47] In the collection *Krieg und Krieger*, edited by Ernst Jünger, op. cit., pp. 51–67, Friedrich Georg Jünger also sees in the alignment of the Soldier with the Worker the major characteristic of modern times. Later, in *Maschine und Eigentum* (*Machine and Property*) (Frankfurt am Main: Klostermann, 1949), he will take up once again, from another perspective, this analysis of the way in which the evolution of technology resulted in total mobilization. Insofar as the "best technology" means an increased chance of victory, every conflict will tend in the direction of "technological perfection."

portrait before photography, the reappropriation of the mask for "utilitarian" purposes, the importance assumed by the *plan* in the life of nations, the alignment of the values of national currencies, the uniformization of production, the proliferation of statistics and typologies, the fixity of faces ("metallic" in the case of men, "cosmetic" in that of women), the restrictions to individual freedom brought by automation, the convergence of efforts toward economic goals that surpass their own framework, collaboration between military brass and industry, etc. Everywhere "the uniform and the typical are substituted for the unique and the individual." All these facts, let us emphasize, reflect a *positive* development in Jünger's eyes. To evoke the power and importance assumed by machines, he sometimes uses a language evocative of Italian futurism.[48] The uniformization of the world is taken here as equivalent to the wearing of a sort of military *uniform*. Jünger does not see this as a sign of decadence, but as a

---

[48] "What is most characteristic of Jünger," observes Henri Plard, "is to have allied in the richest and most provocative of his writings, *The Worker*, an effectively and passionately reactionary ideology with a modernism that joyfully and fiercely makes a clean sweep of everything that is not technologically up to date" (*Etudes germaniques*, July–September, 1979, pp. 292–93). A parallel could just as easily be drawn between Jünger's development from the First World War to the publication of *The Worker* (1932) and that of the Italian writer Curzio Malaparte from the time of the journal *Conquisto dello Stato* (*Conquest of the State*) and *La rivolta dei santi maledetti* (*Revolt of the Cursed Saints*) (Roma: Casa Editrice Rassegna Internazionale, 1924) to *La technique du coup d'Etat* (*The Technique of Coup d'Etat*) (Paris: Grasset, 1931). This parallel could be extended with Jünger's *The Peace* (1945) and *Heliopolis* (1949) and Malaparte's *Kaputt* (Naples: Casella, 1944). Cf. Arthur R. Evans, Jr., "Assignment to Armageddon: Ernst Jünger and Curzio Malaparte on the Russian Front, 1941–43," *Central European History*, XIV, 4, December 1981, pp. 295–321.

promise for the future: the necessary condition for the annihilation of the type of bourgeois individualism. The Worker, therefore, must not slow down but accelerate this uniformization. Only the death of the individual will allow the Worker to institute his reign. Only destruction allows construction, only decomposition allows for *recomposition* on a higher level.

But the *individual* whose death Jünger joyously proclaims is not entirely identical with the individual *person*. We are speaking of the bourgeois individual (*Individuum*) born of Enlightenment philosophy, cut off from his heritage, his origins, and his belonging, by way of opposition to the personal individual (*der Einzelne*) whose identity remains clearly situated within his organic environment. Jünger defines the individual, moreover, as "the most charming invention of bourgeois sentimentality." We have certainly gotten into the habit of considering the individual as an atom of humanity. But humanity as an entity no more exists than the little particles that are supposed to compose it. The individual is only a component of the *masses*, which are the contrary of the *people*: "The individual and the mass are one and the same thing." We should also remark that Jünger presents the discovery of work as an "element of plenitude and freedom." This freedom is obviously not the abstract freedom evoked by theories of the rights of man; nor does it have anything to do with the affluence produced by economic abundance (which can just as well reveal itself as pure alienation). Just as the figure of the Worker does not have to conform to a moral model, but rather morality must conform itself to this figure, so freedom can only be conceived and established within a deep adherence to all which the figure specifies. (There is no goal to be attained, notes Marcel Decombis, but only an intimate *thrust* that must be obeyed.) When he struggles for freedom, the Worker struggles first of all for the very possibility of his work.

Freedom and work are indissociable. Jünger observes that "man furnishes his maximal energy wherever he finds himself in the service of a command": it is when he gives himself the means to be drawn "from above" that he gives the best he has. Freedom cannot reside in a freeing from all constraint; it cannot legitimate any desire for *secession*. It consists rather in voluntary *adherence* to a figure through which the capacities of each individual can be fully expressed. The path of freedom goes by way of the path of *service*: "One can only have the feeling of freedom if one takes part in a unified life full of meaning" (p. 296). To be free consists in *taking part*, and consequently, "the will to freedom takes on the appearance of the will to work" (p. 65). One is free when one can expend the greatest amount of energy; now, one can only deploy the greatest amount of energy by adherence to the figure that incarnates one's essence. Thanks to this freedom/participation, the Worker can realize his integration (*Eingliederung*) into the general structure that *realizes* his type, an integration that touches all aspects of his character and personality. Man can no longer be considered as a being in himself, but only as an incarnation of the figure which gives him his freedom. Conversely, man is all the freer insofar as he participates in that figure. In the future society that Jünger describes, each person's place will be determined not by birth, nor by fortune, nor by rank, but by the *degree of adequation with the figure of the Worker*. The individual person will be a Worker, or he will be nothing.

We see that Jünger's thought, while it took its starting point in the experience of war, rapidly surpassed that context. When Jünger speaks of the advent of the "material war," he is not making a banal observation on the technical development of military confrontation. He draws from it the idea that the "technological" transformation of war has produced a *break* that henceforth affects all of society—and all of the planet. This break simultaneously marks the end of man borne by a certain image of the gods, and the *titanic* irruption of the elemental into daily life. Ancient religions say that at the origin of present civilization there was a struggle between gods and titans. For millennia, the gods held the titans in check. But we are approaching the twilight of the gods, and the titans are returning. In plain language: the elemental is returning by way of the dominance of extremely powerful technological means.

In this unleashing of the elemental, all the old defenses, all the old attitudes, all the old doctrines become obsolete. The classic forms of political action have also been surpassed. Faced with this situation, the response can only be "vitalist": just as the military defeat of Germany in 1918 can be "transmuted" into victory, life must be "alchemically" *intensified*: a new humanity must transmute all existing forms. Then the reign of the Worker will begin.

Julius Evola summarized the situation well in writing of *The Worker*:

> Jünger's merit in this first phase of his thought is to have recognized the fatal error of all those who think that everything can be reordered, that this new, menacing world, ever progressing, can be mastered or stopped on the basis of the vision of life and values of the preceding era, i.e., bourgeois civilization.[49]

And elsewhere:

> It is like a non-human force, awakened and set in

---

[49] Julius Evola, *Oriente e Occidente* (Milan: Archè, 1982). In English: *East and West: Comparative Studies in Pursuit of Tradition*, ed. Greg Johnson and Collin Cleary (San Francisco: Counter-Currents, 2018).

motion by man, from which the individual-soldier cannot escape; he must measure himself against it, he must become the instrument of mechanics, and stand up to it at the same time—spiritually and not only physically. This is only possible if one becomes capable of a new form of existence, if one forges oneself *qua* new human type which, precisely amid situations what would be destructive for any other, is able to seize an absolute meaning of life. . . . This new human type must take shape—this form capable of actively confronting destructions, i.e., of being more their subject than their object—by accepting the aspects by which one can be led toward a surpassing of all that is merely individual, toward a new, active impersonality, toward a "heroic realism" through which neither hedonism nor eudaemonism are any longer the essential agents of existence. This realism, this impersonality, will once again differentiate the human substance beyond all oppositions, all problems of the bourgeois world and its twilight prolongations.[50]

The important thing for man is not happiness. Nor is it wealth. By being on the same level as the figure, by entering into *resonance* with it, "man discovers his determination, his destiny, and it is this discovery which renders him capable of sacrifice." The Worker, writes Jünger, "does not consider martial order an exception, he makes it into his discipline; and it is this resoluteness which assures him an indisputable superiority." Jünger adds that the figure of the Worker "must be considered as it appears, first, on the

---

[50] Julius Evola, *Le Chemin du cinabre* (*The Path of Cinnabar*), trans. Philippe Baillet (Milan: Archè, 1982), 191–92. In English: *The Path of Cinnabar: An Intellectual Autobiography*, ed. John B. Morgan, trans. Sergio Knipe (London: Integral Tradition, 2009).

historical level as the unknown soldier, and second, as it appears today, as master of the world, as a type possessing the perfection of power only vaguely sensed before now." This acceptance of a life called to become a "parable of the figure" corresponds to what Jünger calls "heroic realism."[51] One can see in it an attitude consisting in cool acceptance of whatever happens, in pushing all processes—even negative ones—to their conclusion, to the point where they *reverse*. The "virtue" of heroic realism, Jünger declares, leads one to put up with anything, so that "even the possibility of total annihilation and the vanity of one's efforts are not able to unsettle one." The key notion here is that of *movement*. Heroic realism is based on a lucidity that, instead of paralyzing action, stimulates it.[52] One thinks of the Nietzschean formula *amor fati*, and also that of Evola: "ride the tiger." The shaping of man and the world then become possible: "the important point is not that we have lived, but that it should once again become possible on earth to live a large-scale life according to elevated criteria." Work, we have seen, consists in impressing forms upon the general chaos of the world. The Worker is a demiurge.

Besides, the "whatever happens" that must be coolly

---

[51] This expression was used for the first time by Werner Best in the collection *Krieg und Krieger* (op. cit.). It quickly became associated with Jünger's thought during the thirties. See Edgar Traugott, *Heroischer Realismus. Eine Untersuchung an und über Jünger* (*Heroic Realism: An Investigation into and about Jünger*) (Ph.D. thesis, University of Vienna, 1936).

[52] Friedrich Georg Jünger will write: "People are greatly mistaken to associate the image of a certain inertia and softness of the will with fatalism: for fatalism does not alter the will at all. A strong-willed man is not weakened because he feels himself an instrument in the hand of an inscrutable higher power; on the contrary, concrete examples teach us that he draws uncommon strength from this." *Orient und Okzident. Essays.* (*East and West: Essays*) (Hamburg: Hans Dulk, 1948), p. 215.

accepted is precisely the reign of the Worker. The opposition between the bourgeois and the Worker does not belong only to the conceptual domain, or to that of typology. A "chronological" or *historical* element enters as well. For Jünger, the advent of the Worker is an ineluctable fatality, an accomplished fact that should occasion neither enthusiasm nor regret: "It has become useless to concern oneself with a reversal of values. It is enough to see the new and participate in it." This replacement of the bourgeois by the Worker, since it is unrelated to the substitution of one class for another, cannot be compared with the manner in which, for example, the bourgeoisie succeeded the ancient aristocracy. The caesura, the "reversal," is deeper. The figure, let us remember, is not produced by history, but is *that which makes it possible for history to happen*. It is "only with the advent" of the Worker, says Jünger, "that the art of politics and sovereignty in the grand style, i.e., on a world scale, becomes realizable" (p. 236). Radically revolutionary in the sense that it closes one epoch just as it opens another, the Worker must not hesitate to resort to force to complete the disintegration of the bourgeois world:

> It is force that will decide the problems of the future. This reign of force will restore to life its simplicity by removing it from the dualism that complicates it, and it will radically suppress the dialectical tensions that we are pleased to establish between the individual and society or between barbarism and civilization.[53]

To mobilize is to be ready and make ready, in the sense

---

[53] For the views of a Frenchman writing at about the same time, see Jean Sépulcre, *La Force, principe de la morale* (*Strength, Principle of the Moral*) (Paris: Payot, 1936).

of the soldier who "makes himself ready" for war. But it is also to make mobile, to *set in motion*. How will the Worker mobilize the world and confront "outdated" modes of existence? He is going to mobilize the world by recourse to *technology*, technology that is itself the cause of "total mobilization." By the same token, through this recourse, technology is going to receive its true meaning. The rise of machinery obsessed Europeans of the time. Consider, for example, Fritz Lang's film *Metropolis* (screenplay by Thea von Harbou), from 1927, or J. L. Duplan's book *Sa Majesté la machine* (*His Majesty the Machine*), published in 1930. Now, according to Jünger, only the Worker enters into a "real" relation with technology; only he is capable of having an *authentic* relation with the "total character of work," which is identical with Being in the sense of Will to Power. Technology is not merely "the symbol of the figure of the Worker" (p. 72), it also represents "the way (*die Art und Weise*) this figure mobilizes the world" (p. 150).

The true *raison d'être* of technology is not to "accelerate progress" but to *intensify power*; technology constitutes "the most powerful and incontestable means of total revolution." Besides, not only is "progress" a chimera, but one would be wrong to think technology is called upon to develop infinitely. It must stabilize around a "point of *perfection*" that marks the maximal extent of its possibilities. It is the same with technology as with all forms: it attains its "perfection" when it develops itself in its totality. ("There is no evolution able to draw from existence more than it holds.") Ernst Jünger emphasizes the positive aspects of this idea of a technological "perfection" in the sense of "completion" (*Vollendung*) that Friedrich Georg Jünger will subsequently explore from its critical side. One day a "simplified" technology will appear, which will realize the perfection of its essence. It alone will permit the Worker to institute his dominion (*Herrschaft*) on earth— but conversely, only the establishment of the reign of the

Worker will allow technology to reach its "perfection."

In refuting the myth of progress, Jünger is attacking the idea that technology is *neutral*; that it is at everyone's disposal, or that it is intrinsically liberating, or, on the contrary, that it is intrinsically oppressive. He emphasizes its mediating, revelatory character. In fact, only those who are truly in accord with the new form of life brought about by technology can find in technology their means of expression and action without becoming enslaved to it. It is indeed only the Worker who can have recourse to technology without falling under its yoke, while the bourgeois is condemned in advance either to be horrified at his own hubris (the myth of the Golem) or to marvel foolishly at the "promise of tomorrow" to which technology will somehow lead. "Jünger compares technology to a language everyone can speak," writes Marcel Decombris, "but which is possessed only by those whose mother tongue it is. Issuing from work, of which it is the result as well as the tool, technology is foreign to the nature of the bourgeois, while it belongs to that of the Worker."[54] This comparison of technology to a *language* is entirely appropriate. The Worker has recourse to a new language, a new *saying*, which is provoked by the upsurge of the elemental; he is confronted with the elemental powers of life precisely insofar as he is given over to the entirety of what is. Technology represents the shaping of these powers; it is equivalent to "the mastery of a language that is valid in the space of work."[55]

By giving rise to the type of man able to dominate it, technology sounds the death knell of the era of the individual. The two phenomena go hand in hand: the man who remains an "individual" can only become the slave of technology. To become the master of technology, one

---

[54] Op. cit.
[55] Jean-Pierre Faye, op. cit.

must rise to the level of active impersonality corresponding to the stage of "heroic realism." The reign of the
Worker is the reign of the man *technologized* by work,
whether he is a peasant, a laborer, or a priest; that is how
technology leads "to a well-defined order, uniform and
necessary" (p. 163). In this way, Jünger responds to his
preoccupation of ten or twelve years before. *Feuer und
Blut* (*Fire and Blood*, 1926) had posed the question of
whether man could dominate the machine and realize his
own purposes through it, whether he could "*direct* fate,
and not suffer it." In *Storm of Steel*, the assault platoon
(*Stoßtrupp*) represented the beginnings of a response to
the challenge raised by "material war." In *The Worker*,
work is also a questioning that is itself its own answer. The
figure of the Worker gives birth to a "technological elite"
that is an extension of the *Stoßtrupp*. In both cases it is a
matter of accepting a process notably characterized by the
disappearance of the individual in order to assure mastery.

The advent of the reign of the Worker, prelude to the
total formation of the *space of work*, is equivalent to the
irruption of the elemental into *bourgeois space*. This event
must consecrate the "minting of a race totally devoid of
equivocation," a "prudent, strong" race "intoxicated with
energy," educated according to the model of the "race" of
soldiers, about which Jünger clearly rejected any sort of
biological understanding.[56] Then the process commenced
by the appearance or *unveiling* of the figure will be complete. Work as a way of life will blossom into a *style* of life.
Art will become the formation (*Gestaltung*) of the world

---

[56] From 1926–1927, Jünger emphasizes that "blood" is a metaphysical concept, not a biological one. In August 1926 he wrote:
"The word *race* is beginning to become just as painful in its current use as *tradition*." This clarification is important for understanding what Jünger means by "will to form a new race" (*Wille
zur Rassenbildung*), an essentially historical enterprise oriented
entirely toward the future.

of work. The Worker will at one stroke put an end both to the bourgeois reign of the individual and to the reign of the proletarian masses. In founding his state, he will "break the legal chains" of bourgeois society, reject the "conceptual utopias" of materialism and idealism, and "make his own being the scale according to which the world is interpreted." Marxism, torn since its origins between its fascination with the bourgeois model and its declared hostility to it, will disappear. The same goes for the old religions. "Technology," notes Jünger, "is as it were the destroyer of all faith in general; consequently, it is also the most decisive anti-Christian power that has ever appeared" (p. 154). He adds: "Between the figure of the Worker and the Christian soul no relation can any longer be maintained other than that between that soul and the ancient images of the gods."

Revealing that technology is not neutral, Jünger also exposes as illusory the very idea of "neutrality." Rather, he legitimates the suppression of neutrality in all domains, notably politics, by announcing the end of the "(supposedly) neutral state," i.e., the liberal bourgeois state.[57] In op-

---

[57] It was with explicit reference to the "total mobilization" evoked by Jünger that Carl Schmitt, in 1931, coined the expression "total state" (*totale Staat*). We find it in several authors of the Conservative Revolution, particularly in Ernst Forsthoff. The "total state" is not the totalitarian state (no more than it corresponds to the Marxist conception of *étatisation*); and it is significant that the National Socialist theoreticians violently attacked this formula, to which they opposed that of the "total party." In Italy, Julius Evola provided a good demonstration of the abyss between the total state and the totalitarian state. The former is a supple, living, organic entity; it marks the beginning of a cycle. The latter is a fixed, petrified, mechanized entity; it marks the end of a cycle. While the total state demonstrates no dissociation of its parts, the totalitarian state simultaneously manifests tendencies to atomization and levelling; social relations assume

position to parliamentary democracy and socialist democracy, Jünger gives the name "state democracy" (*Staatsdemokratie*) to the society destined to *figure* the total space of work, a society of "pyramidal" form founded on the "Prussian" principle of command, but within which "the leader is only distinguished because he is the first servant, the first soldier, the first Worker" (p. 39). (Which resolves the problem of despotism: "The Worker does not know dictatorship, since for him freedom and obedience are one.") A tripartite scheme defines its general structure. Jünger distinguishes a first level, subject to exercising the economic function, and which by its homogeneity *passively* realizes the image of the figure; a second level in which the active type is incarnated, specially charged with training and personnel; and finally, a third, sovereign level whose "action directly expresses the total character of work," and whose "imperial-style" authority realizes the figure "in its pure state." This tripartition, we may remark, appears to be an adaptation of a very ancient schema to which the three "estates" (*Stände*) of the German political tradition in some measure correspond.

In *Total Mobilization*, the perspective opened by Jünger remained essentially national: only the German people was declared capable of confronting itself, of mobilizing itself *qua* German. The text ends, moreover, with these revealing lines:

> At a deeper level than the domains where the dialectics of the ends of war apply, the German met a more powerful force: himself. Thus, that war was for him also and above all an occasion for self-realization. This is why the new organization that

---

a mechanical or bureaucratic character; it is the ultimate stiffening of an already dead state that thus hopes to prevent its own decomposition.

has been commanding for a long time already must be a mobilization of that which is German—and of nothing else.

In *The Worker*, on the contrary, Jünger abandons any classically nationalist vision and immediately situates himself in a universal perspective. For a time, he says, nations will become "planned spaces," after which the advent of *planetary* dominion by the figure will realize the overcoming of "all warlike and peaceful processes of work." At the end of a "life or death" struggle, the generalized institution of *Arbeitertum* will put an end to the "Western nihilism" engendered by the reign of the Bourgeois. "Sovereignty of the grand style," as we have seen, can only be exercised "on a world scale." This orientation is important for understanding the positions Jünger will later take concerning the "universal state." Man, as Nietzsche foresaw, has arrived at the historic moment where he has no choice but to either renounce his humanity or to take charge of "mastering of the earth."

III.

Louis Dupeux rightly mentions, in his book on National Bolshevism, the "uneasiness" that surrounded publication of *The Worker* in Germany. "Neither the National Socialists nor their enemies could exploit it," Jünger himself would note.[58] We must remember that the book was like nothing seen before. At the very moment National Socialism was beginning its inexorable rise, this book dismissed racism and anti-Semitism. In an age when nationalist movements defended the rural world and individual differences, *The Worker* called for the suppression of the individual and unreservedly glorified technology as all-

---

[58] Letter to Henri Picard.

powerful. In this context of bitter political struggle, the book distanced itself radically from all existing forms of politics. It deliberately adopted the perspective of the disappearance of the framework of the nation, a supposition altogether unimaginable for the commentators of the time. Finally, if to a certain degree it took a Marxist point of view, this was in order immediately to surpass all Marxism's limitations. Apart from Nietzsche's influence, *The Worker* was not easily recognizable in terms of existing ideas.[59] Those who remembered the talented chronicler of

---

[59] One of Jünger's *maîtres à penser* at the time he was writing *The Worker* was, in fact, the philosopher Hugo Fischer, a little-known figure, but one who played an important role in the intellectual evolution of the author of *Storm of Steel*. Born in 1897, Fischer followed the lectures of the biologist Hans Driesch at Leipzig at the same time as Jünger. In 1935 he also accompanied Jünger to Norway, a country from which he emigrated to England. His principal work, *Lenin: Machiavelli of the East*, which was to appear in 1933 from the Hanseatische Verlagsanstalt, Hamburg, was suppressed for political reasons and did not appear until 1962. Hugo Fischer died in May 1977. See Armin Mohler, "Er war Ernst Jüngers sagenhafter Magister" ("He Was Ernst Jünger's Legendary Master") *Die Welt*, May 13, 1975. He produced several other books, including: *Hegels Methode in ihre ideengeschichtlichen Notwendigkeit* (*Hegel's Method in its Intellectual-Historical Necessity*) (Munich: C. H. Beck, 1928); *Erlebnis und Metaphysik* (*Experience and Metaphysics*) (Munich: C. H. Beck, 1928); *Nietzsche Apostata* (*Nietzsche the Apostate*) (Erfurt: Kurt Stenger, 1931); *Karl Marx und sein Verhältnis zu Staat und Wirtschaft* (*Karl Marx and his Relationship to the State and the Economy*) (Jena: Gustav Fisher, 1932), etc. This last work presents Marx as a critic of modernity, who conceives modernity essentially as alienation. On the same theme, see Ernst Nolte, the "Conservative Features in Marxism," in *Marxism, Fascism, Cold War* (Assen: Van Gorcum, 1982), pp. 22–30.

Hugo Fischer is also the author of the first monograph devoted to the draftsman A. Paul Weber, *A. Paul Weber, Zeich-*

Die Standarte or *Arminius* were often disappointed. Others took hardly any interest in the book, and this is no doubt why its appearance provoked no decisive responses. "At the end of *The Worker*," says Jünger, "it says that this figure is not limited in any national or social regard, but that it has a planetary character. 'Technology is the Worker's uniform.' This remark was not meant to spare either the Right or the Left."[60]

With the notable exception of the former expressionist poet Gottfried Benn, who saw it as a profound attempt to understand the contemporary world, *The Worker* was rather badly received by the "Right-wing" faction of the Conservative Revolution. In the *Berliner Tageblatt*, Hermann Sinsheimer described the Worker as a "phantom."[61] Hans Bogner, a close associate of Wilhelm Stapel, accused Jünger of "Bolshevism."[62] Such was also the opinion of Max Hildebert Boehm, one of the principal members of Moeller van den Bruck's circle, who violently attacked

---

nungen, Holzschnitte und Gemälde (*A. Paul Weber: Drawings, Woodcuts, and Paintings*) (Berlin: Widerstand, 1936). Weber, who was part of the National Bolshevik tendency, was also closely associated with the Jünger brothers beginning in 1928. He produced two oil portraits of Ernst Jünger done in 1935–36. Coeditor of *Widerstand* and *Entscheidung*, he was the official illustrator of the publisher *Widerstand*. In 1932 he illustrated Niekisch's anti-Hitlerian pamphlet *Hitler—ein deutsches Verhängnis* (*Hitler—A German Fate*) (Berlin: Widerstands, 1932), then, in 1934, he illustrated Friedrich Georg Jünger's *Gedichte* (*Poems*) (Berlin: Widerstand, 1932). He was arrested in 1937 and successively interned at the concentration camps of Hamburg-Fuhlsbüttel, Berlin, and Nuremburg, and released a few months later. On his relations with the Jünger brothers see especially Gerd Wolandt, *A. Paul Weber, Künstler und Werk* (*A. Paul Weber: Artist and Work*) (Bergisch Gladbach: Gustav Lübbe, 1983).

[60] Letter to Henri Plard, *ibid.*
[61] *Berliner Tageblatt*, October 4, 1932.
[62] *Die Neue Literatur*, November 1932.

Jünger in a 1933 pamphlet, *Der Bürger im Kreuzfeuer* (*The Bourgeois in Crossfire*), notably declaring that *The Worker* constituted a "the program of a modified Bolshevism" (*das Programm eines Abgewandelten Bolschewismus*). Jünger's book would, moreover, become the target of hostile comment not only from representatives of the *völkisch* tendency, who were horrified to see all forms of neo-romanticism and rural rootedness considered so many affirmations of "bourgeois values," but also from men like Hermann Rauschning and Oswald Spengler.[63]

Although less comprehensive, but more importantly less of a caricature, the later analysis of *The Worker* by Julius Evola overlaps to some extent with the German neo-conservative point of view. Evola, who had at first thought of publishing an Italian translation of Jünger's book, ended up devoting an essay to it entitled *L'Operaio nel pensiero di Ernst Jünger* (*The Worker in the Thought of Ernst Jünger*).[64] He also refers to it in *Men among the Ruins* and *The Path of Cinnabar*. Essentially Evola attacks the concept of work, which he uses in a discernably narrower sense than Jünger. This concept, says the author of *Revolt against the Modern World*, does not break free from the "demonics of the economy," whether one sees in work an end in itself, a path of redemption or justification, or whether one advocates a "humanism of work," or even if

---

[63] It is well known that Spengler associates the birth of the "World-City" with the dissolution of culture at the stage of "civilization." In this point of view Jünger sees a recourse to criteria no longer valid (*The Worker*, 225). In a letter to Jünger, Spengler reaffirms his conviction that the peasantry is not an obsolete value. See Oswald Spengler, *Briefe, 1919–1936* (Munich: Beck, 1963), pp. 667ff. Spengler will develop this idea in 1933 in *The Year of Decision*.

[64] Julius Evola, *L'Operaio nel pensiero di Ernst Jünger* (Rome: Armando Armando, 1960; 2nd rev. ed., Rome: Giovanni Volpe, 1974).

one is content with associating work with "the myth of paroxysmic productive activism." The "modern superstition of work," which manifests itself in both Left and Right, must be denounced everywhere. "One of the most opaque and plebian aspects of the economic era," writes Evola, "is this sort of self-sadism that consists in glorifying work as an ethical value and essential human duty and conceiving any form of human activity as work." Moreover, it is paradoxical to seek an ethical value in work in an age when technology tends to suppress any genuine quality that might still remain in work. For Evola:

> the word *work* has always designated the lowest forms of human activity, those most obviously economically contingent.[65] It is illegitimate to refer to everything that cannot be reduced to such forms as "work." The appropriate word here is *action*: the action, and not the work, of the leader, explorer, ascetic, savant, warrior, artist, diplomat, theologian, of one who enacts or violates a law, of one guided by a principle or driven by elemental passion, of the head of a company or a great organizer.

From this point of view, Jünger's very choice of the word *Arbeiter* is a "suspicious circumstance," for "this concept essentially belongs to the world of the fourth estate, the lowest caste." Jünger thus remains a prisoner of the "proletarian mentality":

---

[65] Etymologically, *négoce*, an ancient synonym for work whose sense of "commerce, market activity" does not go back farther than the seventeenth century, is merely the "negation of leisure" (Latin "neg-otium"). *Négocier* originally meant not being at leisure, having an occupation, with a clear pejorative undertone.

The proletarian spirit, the spiritually proletarian quality, remains when one is incapable of conceiving a higher human type than the Worker, when one raves about the "ethical significance of work," when one exalts the Workers' State, when one does not have the courage to take a position radically opposed to all these new contaminating myths. . . . Our task consists above all of *deproletarianizing our vision of life*, apart from which everything remains falsified and paralyzed.

Moreover, for Evola, who appeals above all to a spiritual tradition, the metaphysical option of the Worker is insufficiently emphasized. The domination of technology, if it wishes to rise above the elementary level, must be elaborated at a level clearly *above* that of contemporary values, in the realm of pure transcendence. The figure of the Worker remains ambiguous in this regard:

With him (the Worker) one can remain within the closed circle of an interior activism and formation bereft of the transcendental dimension, and which therefore lacks any transfiguring element capable of engendering and legitimizing new and authentic hierarchies.

The accusation of "Bolshevism" brought against Jünger by certain neoconservatives seems at first glance justified by the fact that the National Bolsheviks were almost the only ones who were pleased by *The Worker* when it first appeared. Niekisch, who was familiar with the manuscript before publication, published a very positive review in *Widerstand* in the autumn of 1932 ("On Ernst Jünger's New Book") in which he declared that "Jünger's theses display a troubling similarity to the fundamental doctrines of Marxism." However, this similarity, he added, was only

apparent; in fact, Jünger transcends the sentimental response given by Marxism and "demonstrates in masterly
fashion how, at a fundamental level, one can eliminate, liq-
uidate, the bourgeois spirit." Niekisch concludes: "Jünger is
not a Bolshevik, but in spite of himself he attests to how
greatly Bolshevik Russia accords with the dominant spirit
of the world."[66] This opinion, which was not calculated to
improve Jünger's image in "bourgeois" circles, is itself
questionable and should be understood in the context of
the general problematic of German National Bolshevism.
Moreover, within this movement it was not universally
agreed upon. Jünger's "planetary" point of view was discussed by certain National Bolsheviks, as was the rather
vague character of his positions on questions such as the
"Russian alliance," the concept of property, etc.[67]

Orthodox Marxists were not fooled. Communist leader
Karl Radek was canny enough to write, "Bringing an Ernst
Jünger into the KPD would be more significant than gain-
ing the support of all the new voters." But aside from him,
the Marxists' hostility to the ideas of *The Worker* has not
let up for half a century. Jünger, according to Karl August
Wittfogel, was content merely to christen the activists of
the dominant class "Workers." For Lukács, who classed
Jünger among those responsible for the "destruction of
reason,"[68] the figure of the Worker is nothing but a mysti-
fication of Prussian imperialism, insofar as it lacks all reference to class struggle. Lukács' thesis, which according to
Jean-Michel Palmier "cuts off all authentic access to
Jünger's work," was reprised by Jean-Pierre Faye, whose

---

[66] Ernst Niekisch, "Zu Ernst Jüngers neuem Buche" ("On
Ernst Jünger's New Book"), *Widerstand*, October 1932.

[67] Cf. Louis Dupeux, op. cit., pp. 543–47.

[68] György Lukács, *Die Zerstörung der Vernunft* (*The
Destruction of Reason*) (Neuwied-Berlin: Hermann
Luchterhand, 1962).

hostility toward Jünger is apparently explained by the fact that Jünger's thought was expressly conceived "in terms destined to nullify those of any history interpreted in the language of Marx."[69] This hostility is also found in the Soviet Union, in the work of S. Oduev.[70] For Oduev, whose work is written from start to finish in the inimitable "wooden language" of orthodox Marxism-Leninism, Jünger's work, inspired by Nietzsche, displays a "mythologization of reality" and a "macabre romantic adventurism." The myth of the Worker surreptitiously aims at "surmounting by means of a synthesis the irreconcilable opposition between bourgeoisie and proletariat," and represents a means for "fascism" to "win over the masses with demagogy" with a view to "the realization of its bloody plans."

In "Internal Emigration"

Charged with "Bolshevism" yet rejected by Bolsheviks, who considered it "fascist," *The Worker* faced still more bitter hostility from the National Socialists. The *Völkische Beobachter* published a review by Thilo von Trotha in which the Worker is described as "an abstract monstrosity, a moon-man" (*ein abstraktes Monstrum, ein Mondmensch*).[71] Jünger was reproached for his unequivocal rejection of the entire blood and soil ideology. Von Trotha goes so far as to write that the author of *The Worker* is approaching the "headshot zone" (*in die Zone der Kopf-schüsse*).

As Jean-Michel Palmier has said, National Socialism is a movement "to which Jünger will remain always foreign

---

[69] Jean-Pierre Faye, *"L'archipel total"* ("The Total Archipelago") in Lion Murard and Patrick Zylberman, eds., *Le soldat du travail*, op. cit., p. 17.

[70] S. Oduev, *On Zarathustra's Paths: The Influence of Nietzsche's Thought on German Bourgeois Philosophy* (Moscow: Progress Publishers, 1980), pp. 208–42.

[71] *Völkische Beobachter*, October 20, 1932.

and openly hostile." From 1925 on, Jünger criticized the NSDAP which, two years after the failed Munich Putsch, was just beginning to gain ground. In January 1927, addressing an assembly of the Tannenbergbund, he once again clearly emphasizes the differences between National Socialism and neo-nationalism. That same year, Hitler, who admired Jünger's talent as a frontline writer, proposed that he stand as a candidate, under the banner of his party, seeking a term as a Reichstag deputy. "I consider it more meritorious," Jünger responded, "to write a single good line of verse than to represent 60,000 fools [*Trottel*]"! Two years later, Jünger, who wholeheartedly supported the peasant revolt in Schleswig-Holstein, was disturbed to see the NSDAP offer a reward for the capture of the movement's "bomb setters." This position, dictated by a legalist bias, was also that of the Communists. In a powerful article, Jünger declared this proof of the fundamentally "bourgeois" character of these two supposedly revolutionary parties, which were in fact incapable of understanding the gravity of the problems which confronted the peasant movement.[72] At about the same time, Jünger unequivocally criticized Nazi racialism and anti-Semitism,[73] which earned him a violent attack from Goebbels' journal *Der Angriff*.

In *The Worker*, Jünger clearly associates National Socialism with what he calls "musealogical thinking" (*das museale Denken*; thinking associated with the Muses). Following the example of many other representatives of the Conservative Revolution, he condemns the "plebeian style" of the Hitlerist movement, its adulation of the masses, its recourse to "electoral opportunism" and "dem-

---

[72] "'Nationalism' and Nationalism," *Das Tagebuch*, September 21, 1929.

[73] See "Reinheit der Mittel" ("Purity of Means"), *Widerstand*, October 10, 1929.

ocratic parliamentarianism," its *völkisch* mysticism, its banal "biologism," its lack of any real ideology—indeed, its anti-statism and pan-Germanism. This critique is both *conservative* and *revolutionary*. For Jünger, a *historical* politics on a world scale is by nature incompatible with racialism. "To aim at once at world hegemony and at a politics of race, as Hitler wanted to do," he writes:

> is the purest absurdity. One can have different opinions on racial problems. In any case, one cannot mix racialism and its contrary. The way Hitler let himself be obsessed by it was not only the essential cause of the failure of his plans: from the beginning it clearly bore witness to his lack of imperial substance.[74]

Moreover, Jünger is entirely alien to the mystique of the "great man." He believes the Age has need not of a charismatic *Führer*, but of a new type of collective man.[75] In 1954, Evola will express a related sentiment:

> Everything which resembles tyranny, despotism, Bonapartism, the dictatorship of tribunes of the people, is nothing but a degeneration or an inversion of a system based on the principle of authority.

Jünger's attitude to the National Socialist Revolution of 1933 has sometimes been compared to Joseph de Maistre's attitude to the French Revolution of 1789, or to Aleksandr Solzhenitsyn's views on the Russian Revolution of 1917. This parallel does indeed link three "conservative" au-

---

[74] *The Gordian Knot*, 1953.

[75] Beginning in 1930, Jünger also condemned Italian fascism as a final form of bourgeois liberalism (cf. *Die Kommenden*, September 19, 1930).

thors, but their "conservatism" is in reality of a very different nature. While Maistre and Solzhenitsyn can clearly be considered "counter-revolutionaries," Jünger in the 1930s purports to be the partisan of a *different* revolution, and if he considers National Socialism the anti-metaphysical solution *par excellence*, his main reproach to Hitler is not so much for being a "revolutionary" as for being a soulless "petty bourgeois" who committed the German Revolution to a totalitarian path with no escape.

So, when Hitler came to power in January 1933, Jünger's position was unambiguous. Leaving Berlin to take up residence in Goslar, he joined the "internal emigration" and henceforth abstained from any form of political action. However, like Carl Schmitt, he did openly attend receptions held at the Soviet embassy. During the course of 1933, invited to participate in the Deutsche Akademie der Dichtung that the new regime wished to create, he drily refused. Goebbels ordered the press to remain silent about this refusal. Shortly thereafter, Jünger's apartment was searched. The writer was criticized for his associations with Niekisch, but nothing was found to justify his arrest. In 1934, Jünger published *Blätter und Steine* (*Leaves and Stones*); in 1936, *African Diversions*; in 1938, the second version of *The Adventurous Heart*.[76] At the same time, the regime attempted to exploit the writings of his youth. (In 1934, Jünger would write to the *Völkische Beobachter* to protest the publication without his authorization of an extract from the first version of *The Adventurous Heart*.) On September 1, 1939, the very day hostilities began,

---

[76] Ernst Jünger, *Afrikanische Spiele* (Hamburg: Deutsche Hausbücherei, 1936); *Das abenteuerliche Herz. Figuren und Capriccios*, 2nd ed. (Hamburg: Hanseatische Verlagsanstalt, 1938); in English: *The Adventurous Heart: Figures and Capriccios*, ed. Russell A. Berman, trans. Thomas Friese (Candor, NY: Telos Press, 2012).

Jünger published *On the Marble Cliffs*.[77] Printing was halted in 1940 after 35,000 copies had already been sold. "I would give nearly all the literature of the past ten years for this one book," Julien Gracq would say.[78] Jean-Michel Palmier would see in it "the most courageous and profound critique of Nazism made by a German author who did not emigrate, who was still living on German soil." Nineteen forty-two saw the publication of *Gardens and Streets*.[79] When Jünger refused to suppress the passages judged "out of place,"[80] the book was banned in Germany in 1943. According to Karl O. Paetel, *On the Marble Cliffs* and *Gardens and Streets* constituted the two most significant anti-National Socialist documents published under the Third Reich.

In fact, beginning in 1941–42, Jünger was practically forbidden to publish. Among the regime's officials, Bormann and Rosenberg especially expressed a real hatred for him. Hitler, whose lack of sympathy for the philosophy of *The Worker* is confirmed by Rauschning, seems for his part never to have wavered from a certain admiration for

---

[77] Ernst Jünger, *Auf den Marmorklippen* (Hamburg: Hanseatische Verlagsanstalt, 1939). In English: *On the Marble Cliffs*, trans. Stuart Hood (New York: New Directions, 1947).

[78] Julien Gracq, *La littérature à l'estomac* (Paris: José Corti, 1950).

[79] Ernst Jünger, *Gärten und Strassen. Aus den Tagebüchern von 1939 und 1940* (*Gardens and Streets: From the Diaries of 1939 and 1940*) (Berlin: Mittler & Sohn, 1942). Reprinted in the first volume of *Strahlungen* (Tübingen: Heliopolis, 1949).

[80] Hans Speidel, Rommel's former Chief of Staff, recounts how, having received the order to transmit this demand to Jünger, he refused to carry it out. See Armin Mohler, ed., *Freundschaftliche Begegnungen, Festschrift für Ernst Jünger zum 60. Geburtstag* (*Friendly Encounters: Festschrift for Ernst Jünger on the Occasion of His Sixtieth Birthday*) (Frankfurt am Main: Vittorio Klostermann, 1955), p. 182.

the author of *Fire and Blood* and *Storm of Steel*. For Jünger, Hitler was a sort of "mentor *ex negativo*": "I owe to Adolf Hitler the understanding that I had no business venturing into politics." Speaking of the leader of the Third Reich, Jünger wrote in his journal on April 2, 1946:

> As for those of my writings, like *The Worker* or *Total Mobilization*, that might have helped him escape the sphere of partisan National Socialist thought, they contained nothing he could understand, although he may have borrowed a few formulas, thanks to third parties no doubt, in order to integrate them into his arsenal of slogans.

In April 1941, Jünger, who had participated in the French campaign, was stationed in Paris, where he would remain until August 14, 1944, apart from a visit to the Eastern Front (October 1942–February 1943) and a few leaves of absence in Kirchhorst near Hanover, where his wife and younger son were staying. Jünger kept his journal regularly and worked on the manuscript of *Peace*,[81] which would only appear in 1945 in Amsterdam. Jünger became involved with a number of personalities from the French literary world, particularly Marcel Jouhandeau and Paul Léautaud. Gerhard Heller, who devotes a chapter of his memoirs to Jünger, describes the meetings he attended at the Valentiner brothers' apartment on the quai Voltaire: "Along with Jünger, I met rather regularly with Germans such as Rantzau, Ziegler, Eschmann, or Podewils with whom we spoke quite freely of the developing military

---

[81] Ernst Jünger, *Der Friede: Ein Wort an die Jugend Europas, ein Wort an die Jugend der Welt* (*The Peace: A Word to the Youth of Europe, a Word to the Youth of the World*) (Amsterdam, 1945); in English: *The Peace*, trans. Stuart Hood (Hinsdale, Ill.: Henry Regnery, 1948).

and political situation, for they were all more or less op-
ponents of the regime. French friends came to join us as
well, such as Cocteau or Madeleine Boudot-Lamotte."[82]
He also adds: "Jünger was at the heart of one of the most
active *foci* of the German resistance."[83] This activity did
not pass unnoticed in high places. The day after the assassination attempt of July 20, 1944, Jünger was expelled from
the army.[84] A few months later, his fiftieth birthday was
passed over in total silence by the German press. He declared himself flattered.[85]

Jünger's entourage was treated no better. His brother
Friedrich Georg who, in "Der Mohn" ("Opium"), a poem
published in 1934, described National Socialism in barely
veiled terms as "a childish song of inglorious drunken-
ness," was under permanent surveillance by the Gestapo,
and his apartment was searched several times. When life
in Berlin became impossible for Friedrich Georg, he
moved to Kirchhorst, then to Überlingen on Lake Constance, where he spent the rest of his life. In January 1944,
Jünger's son Ernst, member of a Marine unit, was arrested
and imprisoned at Wilhelmshaven for publicly criticizing
Hitler. When his father came to get him released, he was
sent to the Italian front, where he died in November 1944,
at the age of eighteen, on the "marble cliffs" of Carrera.
Jünger's publisher, Benno Ziegler, was also classed as a
convinced anti-Hitlerist. As for Niekisch, he was (like all
the National Bolsheviks) the object of persecution from
the very beginning of the Third Reich. Arrested by a group

---

[82] Gerhard Heller, *Un Allemand à Paris: 1940–1944* (*A German
in Paris: 1940–1944*) (Paris: Seuil, 1981).

[83] *Ibid.*, p. 168.

[84] In a letter to Benno Ziegler of January 31, 1946, Jünger
would say that the manuscript of *Peace* could be considered in
retrospect as part of the "intellectual preparation for the assassination attempt of July 20."

[85] Letter to Benno Ziegler, February 12, 1945.

of stormtroopers on the night of March 7–8, 1933, he was freed shortly afterwards, but the weekly magazine he edited, *Entscheidung*, was banned. In December 1934, the magazine *Widerstand* was banned as well. Arrested once again in 1937, Niekisch was sentenced two years later to life imprisonment. He was freed in 1945, nearly blind and half-paralyzed.

Just after the war, Jünger was once again prohibited from publishing, this time by the Allies; the prohibition would be lifted only in 1949, the year Jünger published his journal and *Heliopolis*.[86] This scandalous, inexplicable decision is difficult to understand today. In fact, however, it merely reveals to what an extent after 1945 everything in the Conservative Revolution that opposes and distinguishes it from National Socialism had been obscured. The dominant ideology, henceforward clearly egalitarian, tends to confound everything that does not derive from its own principles into a dark, nebulous background, thrusting all that it replaced into historical invisibility. Once this propaganda became engrained, an entire dimension of things became literally incomprehensible. And it is precisely the comprehensibility of that dimension of things that allows one access to a book like *The Worker*. Not only did this work of Jünger's not open the way for National Socialism, it was the latter "that is illuminated by Jünger's work," as Jean-Michel Palmier writes, adding:

> It is not the horizon of Hitler's Germany and the death of technology that ought to make *The Worker* accessible, but this historic figure that ought to allow us to understand how Hitlerist Germany, the reign of the Führer-figure, and the totalitarian state became possible, within the horizon of the comple-

---

[86] Ernst Jünger, *Heliopolis: Rückblick auf eine Stadt* (*Heliopolis: Review of a City*) (Tübingen: Heliopolis, 1949)

tion of the metaphysics of the Will to Power.[87]

Both neoconservatives and National Bolsheviks were deeply mistaken to seek the keys to a transient situation in *The Worker*. H. P. Schwarz more accurately saw in the figure of the Worker a great "political myth" in the Sorelian sense of the term. But even this dimension is still insufficient. Such a book should be examined not in order to find a political program but to recognize in it a metaphysical vision in the proper sense of the term. The Worker knows no frontiers, writes Maurice Schneuwly, or rather he crosses them like so many illusory walls. *The Worker* is in the highest degree an "untimely" (*unzeitgemäss*) book, and that is why it is always timely.

Just one author seems to have understood this, the philosopher Martin Heidegger, with whom Jünger developed a particularly fruitful intellectual relationship through the years. As Palmier also remarks:

> Heidegger was undoubtedly the greatest interpreter of Jünger's thought, and the latter's work is a prolongation, a perpetual variation on the questions Heidegger poses to planetary technology and the man it models and rules.[88]

During the winter of 1939–40 at the University of Freiburg, Heidegger devoted a private seminar to *The Worker*. This seminar, at first kept under surveillance by the authorities, was finally suppressed—a significant suppression in that it associated two key authors in the same censure. (Heidegger was at that time the target of the polemics of the National Socialist philosopher Ernst Krieck.) From the

---

[87] Jean-Michel Palmier, *Les écrits politique de Heidegger* (Paris: L'Herne, 1969).
[88] *Ibid.*

start, Heidegger understood the importance of the work as a "description of European nihilism." *The Worker*, he would say, "undertakes in a different way from Spengler that which all the Nietzschean literature has so far shown itself incapable of; [it] undertakes to make possible an experience of Being as Will to Power." It thereby constitutes a starting point from which "the dialogue with the *essence* of nihilism can once again be illuminated."

Heidegger praised Jünger above all for having torn the metaphysical conception of Will to Power away from the "biologico-anthropological domain that led Nietzsche's development so badly astray." Heidegger's point of view was nevertheless clearly critical insofar as Jünger's thought remained in his eyes too beholden to Nietzsche. It is well known that Heidegger, in regard to the theory of the Will to Power—the will to will, the will that wills itself—condemns philosophies that remain determined by the concept of *value* (Nietzsche was satisfied with substituting the value of "life" for the Platonic values of "sickness" and "death") and that therefore continue, inadvertently, to inscribe themselves within the history of Western metaphysics. Nietzsche believed he was putting an end to Socratic and Christian metaphysics. By "inverting" them (as Marx had "inverted" Hegel), Heidegger held that Nietzsche had merely driven them to their apogee. Heidegger goes so far as to see in Nietzsche the "most unbridled of Platonists." Now, the figure of the Worker is undeniably situated within the perspective opened up by Nietzsche: "The metaphysical view of the figure of the Worker corresponds to the project of the essential figure of Zarathustra within the metaphysics of the Will to Power."[89] *The Worker* thereby "remains a work whose metaphysics is the homeland," corresponding to that "calm being" from which all *changing*, all "mobilized" elements of things can

---

[89] Martin Heidegger, *Questions I* (Paris: Gallimard, 1987).

and must be thought. The figure of the Worker is, in Jünger's own terms, a "metaphysical power"; it corresponds, moreover, to the definition Heidegger gives of the concept of metaphysics as characterized by a *deep identity between that which it grasps and the grasping itself.* If the Worker can mobilize the world by a Will to Power in the form of work, this is because that Will incarnates the fundamental trait of that which has been revealed to Western thought as "Being." Now, this amounts to saying that work is identical with Being. Whence the question posed by Heidegger, of knowing "if and in what measure the essence of Being is in itself the relation to the human being"—or, in still more Heideggerian terms: "Does the essence of the figure [*Gestalt*] come forth in the original domain of the *Ge-stell* [enframing]?"[90] Heidegger answers this question in the negative, for if it were so, the essence of Being would remain the power of human representation—which, according to the author of *Being and Time*, would send us back to metaphysics. Jünger, on the other hand, implicitly responds in the affirmative. Putting man in place of God in a certain sense—while "the *Dasein* in man is nothing human"—he makes of the human being the "determining *subjectum*." And this is precisely the height of metaphysics: transferring to man the idea of God in no way amounts to its suppression or supersession.

So, it is clear that for Heidegger *The Worker* belongs to the phase of "active nihilism." It represents in a visionary manner its "fulfillment"—just as Nietzsche's philosophy represents the "fulfillment" of Western metaphysics. The reign of the Worker is nothing but the *realization of the essence of Western Metaphysics in the omnipotence of world technology.* Referring explicitly to *The Worker*, Heidegger writes: "Work today accedes to the metaphysical rank of that unconditional objectification of all present

---

90 *Ibid.*, p. 219.

things that unfolds its being in the will to will."[91] It is therein that the fundamental interest of the book lies: by describing the metaphysical aspect of the process of "technicization" of the present world, it reveals at the same time the *essence of nihilism*. The total mobilization by which the historic figure of the Worker acquires mastery of the entire earth can be perfectly grasped only through the metaphysics of the Will to Power, of which it marks the "perfection" and therefore the "completion":

> The figure of the Worker, which for Jünger mobilizes the world through technology, must be understood as the historic figure of the completion of metaphysics. It is undoubtedly the final word of the Will to Power. The Worker is not an isolated figure: we must understand him as signifying the being of man within completed metaphysics.[92]

IV.

This is still the dominant way of reading *The Worker* today: to see in it a striking and insightful portrait of the manner in which what dominates our age reveals itself. But, at the same time, we must see it from a new point of view. Re-reading *The Worker* requires that we also interrogate it with regard to the development of its author. After "interior emigration," after the rise and fall of the Mauritanian perversion,[93] Jünger turned to entomology and

---

[91] Martin Heidegger, "Die Frage nach der Technik" (1949), *Vorträge und Aufsätze*, ed. Friedrich-Wilhelm von Herrmann (Frankfurt am Main: Klostermann, 2000); in English: "The Question Concerning Technology," *The Question Concerning Technology and Other Essays*, ed. and trans. William Lovitt (New York, Harper & Row, 1977).

[92] Jean-Michel Palmier, op. cit.

[93] One of Jünger's code-words for totalitarianism—Ed.

literature. Between his projects of 1925–32 and his writings published after 1945, there seems to appear a fundamental break. Many things formerly treated as obvious become the subject of new inquiries. "The farther we go," declares Lucius in *Heliopolis*, "the more our uncompensated loss becomes visible. Everything becomes pale, gray, powdery." In fact, Jünger did not so much renounce action as *interiorize* it. The man of knowledge "assumed control" of the man of power.[94] Jünger noticed that it was more fruitful, but also more disturbing, and perhaps more dangerous, to ask a good question than to think one had a good answer. Like Lucius, he had joined the secret troop of Watchers. This development was not an escape. By standing back in order to get a wider view, Jünger was not *retreating*, but *rising higher*, assuming a certain elevation. The process that he had undergone was one of refinement, of purification. It was an ascension to new heights, accession to a new form of sovereignty—still with something metallic about it, especially as regards style, but a metal tempered for something other than a steel helmet. Accession to a summit, bearing on his face a golden mask.

The pendular oscillations in Jünger's work are well-known: they are not contradictions, but so many alternate procedures for perceiving and getting at the essential. We can distinguish three periods in his work: (1) toward the

---

[94] The dialectic of the "man of power" and the "man of knowledge" has long been developed by Raymond Abellio, especially in the third volume of his memoirs: *Sol invictus, 1939–47* (Paris: Ramsay, 1980). The latter experienced a spiritual "caesura" in the 1940s—what he calls his "second birth"—quite comparable to that which marked Jünger's itinerary. Abellio posits that the emergence of the transcendental ego, a true "assumption within unity," represents the only way to exit "from above" the nihilism at work in the modern world. The dialectic of power and knowledge overlaps with that of the "external man" and the "internal man."

universal state (*The Worker*); (2) *The Universal State* (1960); (3) after the universal state (*Eumeswil*). We can also distinguish three types or figures: the Worker, the Rebel, the Anarch. The stages succeed one another without really effacing what comes before. They enter into "dialogue"; they actualize themselves while mutually correcting one another. Certain principal thrusts appear clearly within this development. The observations Jünger made in 1932 on the nature of the world then revealing itself were never disavowed; on this point, Jünger's sentiment never changed. What did change were the lessons Jünger drew from them. What position should one assume in the face of this modern world, which exhibits *active nihilism*? To this question Jünger would give two responses. First, he would radically change his attitude toward technology, which he would henceforth attack with the same vigor with which he had formerly defended it. Retaining the myth of the universal state, but from a "pacifist" perspective, he would develop an increasingly systematic critique of the omnipotence and omnipresence of machines. This is the epoch of the Rebel. In a second period, Jünger would radically dissociate the figure of the Worker from his "technological uniform." With regard to a problematic that remains unchanged—and even manifests itself in an increasingly urgent way—he would imagine a transformation of the figure at the end of which it might constitute a *remedy* for the unleashing of elemental forces of which it previously served as auxiliary. Faced with the challenge of technology, a challenge henceforward perceived as *negative*, the figure of the Worker could thus assume its former value. In other words, Jünger would no longer propose that men ally themselves with the titans. But he would advocate, for the benefit of men, the return of the gods who alone might be able to put the titans back in chains. The problematic of the Worker was never renounced. It was modified, shifted to a higher level.

Immediately after the war, two things had to be recognized: technology had not created a "new man" gifted with a new form of liberty in accord with his type; instead, it had made a slave of him. And far from having put an end to the power of the "bourgeoisie," technology seems to have consecrated this power and *universalized* its domain. Already in *African Diversions* (1936) Jünger expresses a certain disgust for a depersonalizing technology whose uniformity extends without anything to compensate for it. In 1939, *On the Marble Cliffs* would mark the beginning of a profound reversal that would result in works such as *Heliopolis* (1949),[95] *The Forest Passage* (1951), *The Gordian Knot* (1953), *The Glass Bees* (1957), etc.[96] In Jünger's journal (June 11, 1939), we already read:

> Man has detached himself from his work, which has become autonomous, and we can ever more easily dismiss it or find a substitute for it. We can replace it like a part of a machine, and the results it achieves—indeed, its knowledge—have been projected beyond it and orchestrate the process more than they intervene in it.

This quote sets the tone. Jünger no longer believes that technology exalts the power of man; on the contrary, it

---

[95] Cf. Philippe Baillet, "Mythes et figures dans « Héliopolis » d'Ernst Jünger" ("Myths and Figures in Ernst Jüngers *Heliopolis*"), *Totalité* 2, April–June 1977, pp. 24–35.

[96] Ernst Jünger, *Der Waldgang* (Frankfurt am Main: Vittorio Klostermann, 1951); in English: *The Forest Passage*, ed. Russell A. Berman, trans. Thomas Friese (Candor, NY: Telos Press, 2013); *Der gordische Knoten* (The Gordian Knot) (Frankfurt am Main: Vittorio Klostermann, 1953); and *Gläserne Bienen* (Stuttgart: Ernst Klett, 1957); in English: *The Glass Bees*, trans. Louise Bogan and Elizabeth Mayer (New York: Noonday Press, 1961).

diminishes his power. Technological thought of the analytical and rationalist type has proven itself enormously *reductive*. Technology is the vehicle of a blind "*accidental fatality*" that governs both the life and death of men.[97] Everywhere the *mechanical* is substituted for the *organic*; everywhere mere *dynamism* replaces ancient *rhythms*. It is often in mid-course, says Jünger, that historical epochs assume their typical character. Our own epoch revealed itself fully about the beginning of the 1940s. Earlier on, the landscape was only modified here and there: the arrival of radio, motor vehicles, cubism, etc. The two wars catalyzed everything. Now "the world style is becoming visible. . . . Another time is at hand; it is a new epoch." The postwar texts in which Jünger expresses his acquired allergy to technology are innumerable. This is how we must explain the voyages that the author of *The Hourglass Book* (1954)[98] made with increasing frequency over the years: "I am constantly running off to discover virgin lands. But even in New Guinea everything is American. . . . The earth

---

[97] In *Der Kampf als inneres Erlebnis* Jünger had already made this remark: "Every technology is a function of chance and the devices of which one disposes. The bullet is blind, its course involuntary . . ." But this chance character is not yet perceived negatively; instead, it comes under a classical concept of *fatum*. Moreover, Jünger added: "But man carries within himself a *will* that is expressed in storms where explosives, fire, and steel are piled up." Here as well, Jünger's thought evolved. The second essay of the volume *Zahlen und Götter* (*Numbers and Gods*), "Philemon and Baucis" (Stuttgart: Ernst Klett, 1974), is dedicated to the memory of the Austrian legal philosopher René Marcic who died in a plane crash in October 1971. This *technologically accidental* death made a strong impression on Jünger. It was no longer a tragic fact bound up with individual gestures and acts, but a purely *serial* incident.

[98] Ernst Jünger, *Das Sanduhrbuch* (Frankfurt am Main: Klostermann, 1954).

has become a planet of machines." In 1978 once again, Jünger would confide his aversion "for machines in general" to Jean Plumyène.[99]

In *The Gordian Knot*, Jünger returns to the idea of a fundamental antagonism, which henceforth he perceives clearly, between the elemental forces always ready to be unleashed. These are, on the one hand, titanic powers as immense as they are shapeless, *wild* powers without limit, devoted by way of "the demonic" to brutal destruction, and, on the other, a luminous element, divine in the proper sense, represented by a will that establishes order in the midst of chaos and by the power of the spirit. Jünger crystalizes this antagonism in a symbolic way in the age-old confrontation between Asia and Europe: the former corresponding to the elemental forces, while the spiritual power embodied by the latter is represented by Alexander's sword which cut the Gordian knot. But it was not Jünger's purpose to give the conflict he evokes any genuinely geopolitical or intercultural resonance. The two tendencies exist within each civilization, and probably also within each man.[100]

With regard to the individual, Jünger also modified his position. Technology being tied to statism and a kind of collective life, freedom appeared to him increasingly an affair of the solitary man. "The bond of technology can be broken, and precisely by the individual," he writes in *The Forest Passage*. However, this individual was not exactly the same one he attacked in *The Worker*. The Rebel bears

---

[99] "Du côté de Wilflingen," *Magazine littéraire*.

[100] As Evola remarks, the antagonism in question represents an "antithesis of universal spiritual categories that have no necessary relation with particular peoples, civilizations, or continents." It refers "not to a historical Asia, but to an Asia latent as a possibility in each person" ("Orient e Occident: *Der gordische Knoten*," *Orient e Occident*, p. 62). However, Evola makes the mistake, in our view, of thinking that Jünger takes his own comparison literally.

no resemblance to the bourgeois. Who is he? The one who, "deprived of his homeland by the march of the universe" and finally "delivered over to nothingness," continues resolutely to resist and is thereby "brought by the law of his own nature into relation with freedom." He who voluntarily chooses to withdraw from a world where the perversity of technology reigns and affirms the irreducibility within man of every non-measurable value. Thus, freedom remains at the center of Jünger's thought but crystalizes in a different way. The dialectic of the Worker and the Rebel is substituted for the dialectic of the Worker and the bourgeois. Now, in a world where the freedom of refusal is systematically limited, this latter can only be a "solitary walker" (*Einzelgänger*), a "forest walker" (*Waldgänger*). The "return to the forests," an old Germanic tradition, constitutes a "new response of freedom"—keeping in mind that the *Holzwege* of these forests can just as well be the alleyways of large cities.

Later, Jünger would even incorporate in this critique of technology the notion of the "universal state." His development of this point, however, would be slower. In 1960 he published *The Universal State*,[101] a work frequently considered to represent an extreme conversion to universalism and, in that respect, as the work most opposed to *The Worker*. Looked at closely, this opposition is altogether relative. The universal state is, as we have seen, implied in the Worker's reign. After the war, Jünger at first thought it possible to maintain the perspective of the planetary state in a different orientation, contrary to technology and the reign of the Worker. But he ended by renouncing this. From this point of view, his declaration to Jean-Louis de Rambures is significant: "The universal state, and technology along with

---

[101] Ernst Jünger, *Der Weltstaat. Organismus und Organisation* (*The Universal State: Organism and Organization*) (Stuttgart: Klett-Cotta, 1960).

it, are in my view fatal to the individual."[102]

THE PERFECTION OF TECHNOLOGY & THE IDEOLOGY OF THE MACHINE

As is well known, the development of Jünger's ideas on technology is in very large measure bound up with the works his brother published on the subject. Technology is, in fact, a recurrent theme in Friedrich Georg Jünger's works. See especially *Der Missouri* (*The Missouri River*) a book of poems published in 1940. But Friedrich Georg explored technology most thoroughly in a fundamental essay entitled *Die Perfektion der Technik* (*The Perfection of Technology*).[103] This book was written during the spring

---

[102] *Le Monde*, June 20, 1978.

[103] Among Friedrich Georg Jünger's other essays, besides *Die Perfektion der Technik*, the most important titles are *Über das Kosmische* (*About the Cosmic*) (Berlin: Widerstands-Verlag, 1936), *Orient und Okzident* (*East and West*) (Hamburg: Dulk, 1948), *Maschine und Eigentum* (*Machine and Property*) (Frankfurt am Main: Klostermann, 1949), *Nietzsche* (Frankfurt am Main: Klostermann, 1949), *Rythmus und Sprache im deutschen Gedicht* (*Rhythm and Language in German Poetry*) (Stuttgart: Klett, 1952), and *Sprache und Kalkül* (*Language and Calculation*) (Frankfurt am Main: Klostermann, 1956). Friedrich Georg Jünger also published numerous collections of poems of a classical craftmanship influenced by Goethe, Hölderlin, and Klopstock: *Der Krieg* (*The War*) (Berlin: Widerstands-Verlag, 1936), *Der Taurus* (*Taurus*) (Hamburg: Hanseatische Verlagsanstalt, 1937), *Der Missouri* (*The Missouri River*) (Leipzig: Insel, 1940), *Der Westwind* (*The West Wind*) (Frankfurt am Main: Klostermann, 1946–47), *Das Weinberghaus* (*The Weinberg House*) (Hamburg: Dulk, 1946), *Iris im Wind* (*Irises in the Wind*) (Frankfurt am Main: Klostermann, 1952), *Ring der Jahre* (*Ring of Years*) (Frankfurt am Main: Klostermann, 1954), etc. In 1950 he received the Literature Prize of the Bavarian Academy of Fine Arts, which was followed by the Immermann Prize (1952), the Bodensee Literature Prize (1955), the Literature Prize of the Kul-

and summer of 1939. Its first recorded title was *Die Illusion der Technik* (*The Illusion of Technology*). No sooner was it finished than it fell victim to that which it denounced. The plates were destroyed in 1942 in the course of a bombing raid on Hamburg. The first edition was then reduced to ashes in 1944, also the result of a bombing raid, so that the

---

turkreises der deutschen Wirtschaft (Baden-Baden, 1956), the Wilhelm Raabe Prize (1957), and finally the North Rhein-Westphalia Grand Prize for Literature (1960). In 1963 he received the Bundesverdienstkreuz. Coeditor of the journal *Scheideweg* (*Crossroads*), which is still published by Vittorio Klostermann, F. G. Jünger took a great interest in the philosophy of science toward the end of his life, especially the philosophy of biology. See, for example, *Die volkommene Schöpfung. Natur oder Naturwissenschaft?* (*The Coming Creation: Nature or Natural Science?*) (Frankfurt am Main: Klostermann, 1969). In 1969, at age 71, he published a new translation of the eleventh book of the *Odyssey*. He died at Überlingen, on Lake Constance, on July 20, 1977, after having recounted his life in two volumes of memoirs: *Grüne Zweige* (*Green Branches*) (München: Hanser, 1951), which stops in 1926, and *Spiegel des Jahres* (*Mirror of Years*) (München: Hanser, 1958). His complete works are currently being published by Klett-Cotta. A bibliography of his work (as far as August 1958) assembled by Armin Mohler can be found in the edition of a speech delivered by Benno von Wiese on the occasion of his 60th birthday: *Friedrich Georg Jünger zum 60 Geburtstag* (*Friedrich Georg Jünger for his Sixtieth Birthday*) (Munich: Carl Hanser and Frankfurt-am-Main: Vittorio Klostermann, 1958). On F. G. Jünger see also Sophie Dorothee Podewils, *Friedrich Georg Jünger: Dichtung und Echo* (*Friedrich Georg Jünger: Poetry and Echo*) (Hamburg: Dulk, 1947); Franziska Ogriseg, *Das Erzählwerk Friedrich Georg Jüngers* (*Friedrich Georg Jünger's Narrative Works*) (Ph.D. thesis, Innsbruck, 1965); Dino Larese, *Friedrich Georg Jünger. Eine Begegnung* (*Friedrich Georg Jünger: An Encounter*) (Amriswil: Amriswiler Bücherei, 1968); and Anton H. Richter, *A Thematic Approach to the Works of F. G. Jünger* (Bern and Frankfurt-am-Main: Peter Lang, 1982).

work appeared only in 1946.[104]

Its publication was rather coolly received, and it was the object of numerous criticisms. Friedrich Georg Jünger was accused of "romanticism" and "cultural pessimism"; he was represented as a "reactionary" whose critique of technology was more "poetic" than factual. After 1968, however, the work gradually became the object of more nuanced assessments, when it was perceived that the author had broadly anticipated certain ecological and "anti-establishment" points of view.

The central thesis of *Die Perfektion der Technik* can be summarized as follows. Formerly, utopias concentrated on a model of the ideal state. This "utopian material" has today been replaced by the technological element. The rise of machines has occasioned a whole series of beliefs, each more erroneous than the ones that came before. The idea that the arrival of technology has permitted a diminution of labor and an increase in wealth is one of these beliefs. In reality, the progress of technology has, on the whole, never ceased to *increase* the amount of work imposed on man while at the same time radically changing the nature of that work. If man could genuinely enrich himself through production, he would long ago have attained happiness. But true wealth is a matter of *being*, not hav-

---

[104] Ernst Jünger mentions *Die Perfektion der Technik* in his journal on August 14, 1945. The book was published in 1946 by Klostermann. A revised version was published in 1949 (the number of chapters increasing from thirty-nine to forty-six), along with an American translation, *The Failure of Technology*. A third editon in 1953 would include the text of another essay, *Maschine und Eigentum* (*Machine and Property*). The seventh edition appeared in 1980. On this book, see especially Wolfgang Hädecke, "Die Welt als Maschine. Über Friedrich Georg Jüngers Buch, *Die Perfektion der Technik*" ("The World as Machine: On Friedrich Georg Jünger's Book *The Perfection of Technique*"), in *Scheidewege*, X, 1980, pp. 285–317.

ing. Now, the farther the reign of technology extends, the more the world becomes spiritually impoverished, and the more of his humanity man loses. There is no more infallible sign of poverty than the progressive rationalization of the general organization of life. Technology offers no deep joy, no feeling of fulfillment or of being raised up; it merely excites envy, cupidity, and resentment. The rational spirit at work in the machine, and by the same token the machine itself, stimulates appetites that nothing can satisfy. Everywhere the world of technology intensifies anxiety (*Angst*) and the feeling of "strangeness" (*Unheimlichkeit*). Correspondingly, man becomes even less the master of his universe. He is transformed into a "technomorphic" being. His work, increasingly specialized, increasingly dissociated from leisure, becomes itself a repetitive and uniform occupation. Man is enslaved by a technology that constantly generates artificial needs that he must work ever harder to satisfy. Finally, with the help of individualism, he becomes an *object*, a *part* of the technological process. The state itself is "technologized." The entire society becomes a gigantic mechanism.

One of the most characteristic aspects of this "technicization" of thought is the diffusion of a *mechanical concept of time*, without which the type of organization technology has created would be impossible. Time is henceforth *domesticated* by a rational, calculating thought. Yesterday, man mastered time; today, time possesses him. The birth of the mechanical watch marked this development. With it, the man out for a stroll became a "species heading for extinction." We find the same observation in Ernst Jünger, who observes: "no one has time anymore."[105] Just recently, Jacques Le Rider asked Jünger, "What in your opinion were the most significant facts of the twenti-

---

[105] Ernst Jünger, *Subtile Jagden* (*Subtle Hunts*) (Stuttgart: Klett, 1967).

eth century?" Jünger responded:

> The invention of new mechanical watches which re-
> placed all the natural measures of time. These watch-
> es extend their power and become ever more daunt-
> ing. . . . They no longer measure time but fabricate it.
> They do not allow man to dominate time, but subject
> him to their own automatism.[106]

More generally, the sciences themselves transform man
into an *object*. Intended to discover laws that allow the
production of precisely replicated events, concerned
above all therefore with the mechanical recurrence of factors of regulation, they ineluctably enclose man in a net-
work of determinations. Man is no longer the "measure of
all things"; he *gets measured according to all things*. Thus,
everywhere reigns an impulse that tends toward technology's point of perfection (*Perfektionstrieb*). This "perfection of technology" corresponds to the moment when all
sectors of existence will be rationally and mechanically
organized, where social "transparence" will be totally realized, where a functionalism and perfect automatism, from
which nothing can escape, will reign supreme. This tendency is today the principal fact about the world. The
reign of technology transcends, indeed, anything that distinguishes East from West. "Capitalist machinism and
Marxist machinism are brothers," explains Friedrich Georg
Jünger. Both are *ideologies of the machine*.[107] Here again
we find the same opinion in Ernst Jünger:

> The two great world powers increasingly resemble

---

[106] *Le Monde Dimanche*, August 29, 1982.
[107] In *Maschine und Eigentum*, Friedrich Georg Jünger explains: The communist learned much from his capitalist brother
and did not go to his school in vain.

one another. When they are flown over by the same satellite, you will see everywhere the same buildings, the same factories, the same nuclear reactors. . . . The great powers, those that want to dominate the world, are forms, modalities of the figure of the Worker. They are converging, and perhaps the World State will comprehend both of them, in a dialectical fashion, if they arrive at a synthesis.[108]

But the arrival of technology at its point of perfection also corresponds to its *reversal*. Far from perpetually engendering new "progress," technology, once it has passed a certain threshold, tends to annul itself, to reduce itself to a succession of adjustments of detail of a purely technical nature. The hypertrophy of an ideology of productivity gives way to a *counterproductivity* in all domains, then to *unproductivity* pure and simple. This is what happens in *Heliopolis*, where technology becomes dormant after having attained its ends, or in *Eumeswil*, where it is marginalized in a certain fashion after nearly giving way to magic. The "perfection of technology" in this sense is also the end of history.

In short, far from issuing in the liberation of man, the reign of technology brings about his slavery and the devastation of the life of the spirit. As for the planet, it suffers a generalized plundering. For the spirit of calculation, the earth can only in fact be an *object of relation*, a dead sphere devoted to exploitation, of which the *maximum* possible use must be made. In fact, the machine destroys everything. It massacres landscapes, pollutes the environment, constantly forces the countryside to give way to increasingly dangerous, ugly, and uninhabitable large cities. Generalized exploitation brings about generalized

---

[108] Interview with Jean Plumyène, *Le Magazine littéraire*, June 1982.

desolation. The utilitarian structures of industry become the general rule. The man of technology is only interested in technology and has little or no interest at all in its effects on man himself. The world of today is one of disintegration and atomization. The dichotomies between being and having, between knowing and doing, become starker each day.

This analysis by Friedrich Georg Jünger, which Ernst Jünger makes his own, seems in total contradiction to the views expressed in *The Worker*. On many points, the contradiction is real. However, Jünger remains faithful to the *problematic* he posed. It is still a matter of knowing how man can remain master of himself, how he can remain a *creator of forms*. In *The Worker*, the bourgeois was described as deriving from a principle totally antagonistic to the spirit of technology. Since then, it has turned out that the bourgeois is *bound up with* technology, which, moreover, began its rise with the philosophy of the Enlightenment. We observe that Jünger—after the war just as in 1932—*never sides with the bourgeois*. His critique of technology is itself a critique "from above," never "from below," nourished on a naïve individualism or defense of weakness. At most, his development perhaps testifies to the deeply ambiguous character of a technology that, depending on whether it is or is not subject to a will strong enough to *appropriate* it, can just as well be the best of things, as well as the worst. This problem of the *nature of technology* is obviously fundamental. One thing is certain: the relations between man and technology do not escape the dialectic of the master and slave. Technology, as we have seen, is never neutral: either man dominates it, or he is dominated by it. In his journal, Jünger writes that after the First World War, the question was whether man or machine would prove the strongest. In *Peace*, he declares that technology must be subordinated to divine and human forces. Today the question remains: is it men or machines who will dominate the world?

"AN ASSURED & IMPERTURBABLE MARCH"

Jünger never stopped posing this question; only the answers he gave changed. And that is why the figure of the Worker always obsessed him. In his journal for August 9, 1942, he notes: "For years I wanted to write a second version of *The Worker* that will probably never see the light of day." A few days later, August 16, he once again mentions "certain revisions" he would like to make to his book. On September 16 he mentions *The Worker* as one of the most important works he has written up to that time ("my Old Testament"). On April 30, 1943, he writes:

> *The Worker* . . . acts just like an automaton; it has brought me, now and again, both adversaries and partisans whom I find equally disturbing. Its traits are those of a son who absolutely does not want to obey his father. Thus, it demonstrates its relation to the world of technology. It is dear to me, however, for I gave much of my blood to it. For me it is the monument of a debate with the mechanical world. I went through it as one traverses great battles, and it is in this respect that the book remains exemplary, for one cannot escape this world . . .

One year later, March 17, 1944, he mentions a "translation being undertaken" of *The Worker*; it was never to appear. On December 7, 1944, he is still thinking of taking up the book again or completing it with a "theological part." This "complement" would in fact appear twenty years later in the form of a small collection of notes and additions to *The Worker* entitled *Maxima-Minima*.[109]

---

[109] *Maxima-Minima* was republished by Klett-Cotta (Stuttgart, 1983).

Jünger's seeming to distance himself from *The Worker*
should not delude us. For half a century, Jünger never lost
sight of just how far the figure of the Worker remains *present* among us. On June 10, 1945, a few weeks after the defeat of Germany, he writes of it:

> Catastrophes cannot hold up his march. They favor
> it, rather, and advance it for the simple reason that
> they break the chain of economics, while the figure
> progresses, invulnerable, across the world of fire,
> endowed with a spiritual power that grows con-
> stantly. So, we can foresee further great realizations.

Once again, in *The Forest Path*, he asserts that the figure
of the Worker "progresses toward his goals with an imper-
turbable step."

> The fire of annihilation merely highlights the splen-
> dor of it. It shines yet with the uncertain brightness
> of the Titans; we do not suspect in what residences,
> what cosmic metropolises, it will raise its throne.
> The world will bear its uniform and arms, and will
> undoubtedly one day put on its holiday costumes.

Gilles Lapouge interprets this remark as follows: "Yes, the
figure of the Worker remains for me the most important.
He is the only unalterable figure."[110]

But from where does the Worker take his "unalterable"
character? What is the secret of his irresistible advance?
In *An der Zeitmauer* (*At the Wall of Time*, 1959),[111] Jünger
observes that the figure of the Worker is:

---

[110] *La Quinzaine Littéraire*, February 16, 1980.

[111] Ernst Jünger, *An der Zeitmauer* (Stuttgart: Klett-Cotta,
1959).

the only one we see emerge ever more powerful from each conflagration. . . . This suggests that the elements that can withstand fire are hidden within it, and that it has not yet found its pure casting.

From this consideration, a new idea comes to light: the idea that the Worker (and work itself) is not ineluctably bound to technology. Carrying out a new revision of this work, Jünger asks himself whether it is possible to *conceive the Worker apart from technology*. Certainly, as he has written, technology is the "Worker's uniform." But one can *change uniforms*. We find this thought in the journal for August 14, 1945:

If the figure of the Worker is incarnated, as I am sure it is, in dominating and persuasive personalities, these do not proceed exclusively, perhaps not at all, from the technical order.

However, at this time he still adds:

It is precisely in this way that technology will know the sovereign will. Refined not merely in the sense of domestication, but in that it will be raised to the rank of a theme for art, perhaps of magic as well.

Later on, he would go further. The dissociation of the Worker from technology was carried out radically in the course of the 1960s. In 1977, Jünger declares to Jean Plumyène: "My Worker is only costumed as a Worker thanks to technology." On February 6, 1980, he writes to Walter Pratt: "The economy and technology are merely the fall of the fold which animates the garment [*nur der Faltenwurf, der das Gewand bewegt*]." The same year he makes the following revealing remarks to Gilles Lapouge:

The figure of the Worker is perhaps only bound to the world of technology in a provisional way. Today, technology is his uniform, but one can imagine metamorphoses, and that from an economic figure he could become a *mythical* figure. He will transform technology into a sort of magic. . . . It may well be that technology, which today is confused with the figure of the Worker, is only one moment, an embryonic form, and that other qualities, characters, or equipment of the figure of the Worker are already there, but without yet having begun to function.[112]

This obviously amounts to a fundamental reorientation, one that raises basic questions. Having cast aside the uniform of technology, does the Worker still merit his name? Does Jünger simply mean to say that besides technology, the Worker can call upon other means to establish his reign (without this changing in any way the assessment Jünger will henceforth make of that reign)? Or is he sketching a sort of rehabilitation of the Worker who, no longer being assimilated intrinsically to the elemental forces of destruction, can by the same token escape the world of the titans to find himself associated with that of the gods? Is it even possible that the Worker can establish himself once again as a *meaning-giving* figure, thus allowing man to escape nihilism and become once again the "princely" measure of all things?

For this is indeed what is at stake. "The true conservative," wrote Jünger in *Maxima-Minima*, "is not one who wants to maintain this or that order, but one who knows how to reaffirm that man is the measure of all things [*sondern das Bild des Menschen wiederherstellen, der das*

---

[112] *La Quinzaine littéraire*, op. cit.

Mass der Dinge ist]."[113] But how can one attain such a goal? How, in other words, can one once again transform a defeat (the "technicization" of the world) into victory? To find some elements of a response to this question, let us turn once more to the work of Friedrich Georg Jünger.

Like the classics of the eighteenth century that look to antiquity for remedies to the evils of their age, and following the example of many other authors of this century (George, Mann, von Hofmannsthal, Rilke, Hauptmann) Friedrich Georg Jünger plunged into the study of *myth*, especially Greek mythology, in search of a key that would allow him better to understand his present situation. A myth, in fact, belongs neither to yesterday nor to tomorrow: it is *eternal*. It is permanently relevant; it speaks to us at any moment. This interest led Friedrich Georg Jünger to publish, over the course of the last thirty-five years of his life, a great number of poems and essays on the ancient world, among which we must particularly cite *Greek Gods* (1943), *The Titans* (1944), and *Greek Myths* (1947).[114]

The world of technology, according to Friedrich Georg Jünger, falls under the *universe of the titans*. In Greek religion, everything involved in the origin and beginnings of technology is attributed to the titans, the most celebrated of whom is Prometheus.[115] Moreover, in antiquity nearly

---

[113] The description "conservative anarchist" given to Jünger by Hans-Peter Schwarz appears rather superficial in this regard.
  See *Der konservative Anarchist. Politik und Zeitkritik Ernst Jüngers* (*The Conservative Anarchist: The Politics and Topical Commentary of Ernst Jünger*) (Freiburg im Breisgau: Rombach, 1962).

[114] Friedrich George Jünger, *Griechische Götter: Apollo, Pan, Dionysos* (Frankfurt am Main: Klostermann, 1943), *Die Titanen* (Frankfurt am Main: Klostermann, 1944), and *Griechische Mythen* (Frankfurt am Main: Klostermann, 1947).

[115] In Germanic religion, the role assigned to the titans devolves upon the giants.

all terms referring to *Homo faber* were pejorative, and certainly not by accident. The more man devotes himself to technology, the farther away he turns from the gods, who are the titans' adversaries. The *titanic* character of technology is observed today in the modern taste for the colossal, for soulless gigantism, in the disappearance of any collective sense of beauty, harmony, and proportion. To the titans are opposed the gods. Those that play the greatest role in the work of Friedrich Georg Jünger are Apollo, Dionysius, and Pan. The second, especially, incarnates a life feeling entirely opposed to the world of technology and calculating reason. Friedrich Georg Jünger uncovers a radical antagonism between the *Dionysian* and *titanic* elements. As opposed to the titans, who symbolize an ever-recurrent negative power, Dionysius represents that which is ever *becoming* in a positive way: the unceasing transformation of the world, the exuberance of life. He is the god of *metamorphosis*. Apollo, on the contrary, is the god of permanence, but also of order and beauty—he who is opposed to chaos, he who "draws the boundaries":

> Since he is the enemy of everything that is shadowy, diffuse, and confused, he emanates a wave of light that illuminates the shadows with a gilded light and creates order. He incarnates the supreme spiritual conscience that gives off a view of the whole and coherence, and is opposed to everything that is unresolved, ambiguous, indecisive. . . . It is the spirituality of form that speaks to us through the intermediary of Apollo, and everything that emanates from him has a noble, fixed form. Form is by definition that which binds the parts into a whole; it is the nature and manner of this assemblage that dominates unformed matter, to which matter bends.

As for Pan, he symbolizes the abolition, the non-existence,

of time. He is the figure who "reconciles" Dionysius and Apollo.

For Friedrich Georg Jünger, as the Greek philosopher Empedocles had already proclaimed, there exists a natural solidarity, an organic *continuity* between life and the universe, between plants, animals, and humans. It is from this continuity that the "enchantment" of the world proceeds. Now, technology, by attacking *distance* (as opposed to "transparence," which it everywhere tries to establish), makes all "enchantment" disappear: "Where there is no distance, everything becomes demonic" (*Wo keine Distanz ist, wird alles dämonisch*), writes Friedrich Georg in *Gedanken und Markzeichen (Thoughts and Hallmarks).*[116] This disenchantment (*Entzauberung*) of the world realized by technology is, as Max Weber saw, part of the prolongation of the philosophy of the Enlightenment and, beyond that, of the struggle of Christianity against paganism. It was begun in the sacrilegious act of St. Boniface in cutting down the oak sacred to Thor, an act that Friedrich Georg Jünger interprets as "contempt, disregard for life" (*Missachtung des Lebens*). In the modern world, the love of nature is related henceforth to a feeling of "protection," of *pity* for something damaged and sullied. This has nothing in common with the ancient feeling of *communion* that formerly bound man and the earth. The earth itself is no longer regarded as a goddess or mother, but as one planet among others, a sphere among the spheres, a pure "object." Relying on the myth of Antaeus, son of the Earth and Poseidon, Friedrich Georg asserts there is nothing of which we have greater need today than to demonstrate once again a true love of the earth.

Friedrich Georg Jünger absolutely refuses to be classified as a "reactionary." Far from preaching any sort of re-

---

[116] *Gedanken und Markzeichen* (Frankfurt-am-Main: Vittorio Klostermann, 1949), p. 83.

treat, he presents a way *through* (*hindurch*) rather than a way *back* (*zurück*). He does not propose to return to any *previous* stage of technology, but rather, relying on what has already been, to "traverse" the technological age, to go through its unfolding to the very end, and to *go beyond*. To the world of technology, he opposes the world of *play*,[117] a cyclical world governed by the notion of "dance" and the idea of festival, where time and space are no longer dissociated, where mechanical laws of causality lose their power, where plural rhythm resumes its rights over the uniform dynamic of "progress." To express this cyclical concept of existence—what stands opposed to the Judeo-Christian tradition of a "directional" history, oriented in advance in a determined direction—he has recourse to the symbols of the dance, running water, and the serpent. Existence, Friedrich Georg says, is not a slice of "history" between two atemporal eternities, nor a uniform movement along a single route, but an "explosion" in all directions, with multiple, indefinitely renewed aspects. The idea of cycle is, in his eyes, Dionysian. He expresses it in a poem, "Die Perlenschnur" ("The String of Pearls"), from the collection entitled *Ring der Jahre* (*Ring of Years*, 1954):

Dies ist immer noch mein Jahresgang
Dies ist meines Kreises Bewegung
Kyklos! Kyklos!
Ich komme und gehe wieder
Und ich komme noch einmal, denn süss ist's.

This is still the year of my birth
This is the movement of my circle
Kyklos! Kyklos!
I come and go again

---

[117] See "Die Welt des Spiels" ("The World of Games"), last chapter of *Die Spiele* (*The Games*) (Munich: List, 1959).

And I come once more, for it is sweet.

On this last point, Friedrich Georg Jünger is close to Nietzsche, to whom he dedicated a book, but without wholly accepting his point of view. If he agrees with the author of *Zarathustra* in the conviction that the idea that "progress" is an absurdity, and that the cycle (or sphere) predominates over the line, he does not perceive the contradiction between "eternal recurrence" and "eternal presence." More precisely, he does not accept that the doctrine of eternal recurrence leads to accepting the *fulfillment* of nihilism as an indispensable precondition of its "overcoming." The way Nietzsche associates the ideas of eternal recurrence and absolute time has in his eyes something negative and disturbing about it. He sees in the Nietzschean eternal recurrence something related to the reign of the titans. He clings instead to an "eternal present" related to the infinite recurrence of Dionysius and Pan. More than a truly "antilinear" conception of time, he proposes a radical *negation* of time.

V.

Niekisch said of Ernst Jünger that he was a "seismograph" who "detected the slightest vibrations and shocks within the social body with the greatest precision." If Jünger is so interested in insects, it is perhaps because he himself possessed antennae. His nature is both visual and intuitive; he *sees things from the inside*—in which respect he is related to prophets and poets. What characterizes the prophet is the nature of the bond that attaches him to the world; prophecy does not come from the intellect but from the soul. Like poets, prophets step back only in order to grasp things and beings *as tightly as possible*. They only seem to go away in order the more powerfully to return. Like those "blind seers"—physically blind, spiritually sighted—who, like Homer, draw from their apparent handicap their real ability, they dominate time because they are above time. Similarly, as Jünger specifies in *Fassungen*, prophets are "the eyes of the people":

> to be in spirit means, for the prophet, being at his post; it is the same thing for him as being at his combat post for the soldier, as being on his throne for the king, as being knowledgeable for the savant. But this leads him well above will, well above domination and knowledge [*science*].[118]

What is it that Ernst Jünger sees? He sees *nihilism*. And it is on this theme, directly tied to that of the Worker, that after the Second World War Jünger will once again enter into dialogue with Heidegger.

The two men met face to face only after the war. (Heidegger was among the first to advise Jünger to have *The Worker* republished.)[119] To these meetings there was soon added an intellectual exchange destined to leave its mark. In 1950, Jünger dedicated to Heidegger, on the oc-

---

[118] Ernst Jünger, *Fassungen*, vols. I–III (Stuttgart: Klett-Cotta, 2015).

[119] On the relations between Jünger and Heidegger, cf. especially Wolfgang Kaempfer, *Ernst Jünger* (Stuttgart: J. B. Metzler, 1981), pp. 119–28: "Die Phänomenologie des Nihilismus. Zur Nihilismus Diskussion Jüngers mit Heidegger"). This subject was also treated during the international congress of Jünger studies held in Rome at the Goethe-Institut March 14–16, 1983. On this occasion, Cesare Casès, a disciple of Lukács, gave a presentation on *The Worker* and "romantic anti-capitalism." Another presentation, by Massimo Cacciare, "Tecnica e nihilism. Jünger und Heidegger," was published in the review *Elementi* (March–April 1983, pp. 41–44). On this conference, cf. Alfredo Cattabiani, "Ernst Jünger, un testimone del nichilismo occidentale," in *Il Tempo*, March 14, 1983; and "Il nuovo operaio secondo Jünger," in *Il Tempo*, March 17, 1983.

casion of his sixtieth birthday, a text entitled "Über die Linie" ("Across the Line")[120] A few years later, Heidegger responded with an essay bearing almost the same title, "Über 'die Linie,'" ["Regarding 'the Line'"] which was first published in *Friendly Encounters*[121] before being republished in 1959 under the title "Zur Seinsfrage: Über 'die Linie'" ("On the Question of Being: Regarding 'the Line'").[122] It mainly discusses nihilism.

Jünger's text is above all a meditation based on Nietzsche and Dostoevsky. Faithful to the viewpoint sketched by Nietzsche, Jünger defines nihilism as a generalized destruction of *meaning*, as a process of *reduction* corresponding to the stage where "the highest values lose their value." Seeing in nihilism a "fundamental power," he asks himself how it could be possible once again to bring about the resurgence of a value harmonizing with "the princely appearance of man," given the destruction of all values that this power sets in motion. In this respect, nihilism appeared to him both a destructive factor and a necessary condition for a new construction, as a weakness and a strength, a state as "normal" as it was "pathological." This ambiguous, contradictory character is explained by the

---

[120] Ernst Jünger, *Über die Linie*, 3rd rev. edition (Frankfurt-am-Main: Vittorio Klosterman, 1951). In English: "Across the Line," Martin Heidegger and Ernst Jünger, *Correspondence: 1949–1975*, trans. Timothy Sean Quinn (New York: Rowman and Littlefield, 2016).

[121] Op. cit., pp. 9–45.

[122] In French: "Contribution à la question de l'être," trans. Gérard Granel, in Martin Heidegger, *Questions* I (Paris: Gallimard, 1968), pp. 195–252. In English: "On the Question of Being," trans. William McNeill, in Martin Heidegger, *Pathmarks*, ed. William McNeill (Cambridge: Cambridge University Press, 1998), pp. 291–322. We have translated Benoist's Granel translation into English and also cite the equivalent pages in McNeill.

fact that nihilism, like technology, is destined to annul itself, to *reverse* itself once it reaches a "line" to which Jünger gives the name "zero point" (*Nullpunkt*) or "zero meridian" (*Nullmeridian*). This "line" corresponds to the entry of man into the area of "perfect" or finished (*vollen-det*) nihilism. For now nihilism is the "normal state" (*der normal Zustand*) of the Earth; it is the disquiet that, by spreading, does not even disquiet anyone anymore. It is, as we have seen, the "universal destiny" of the East as well as the West. (From the metaphysical point of view, Heidegger will say, America and the Soviet Union are "the same thing"; both are characterized by "the same sinister frenzy of unbridled technology and rootless organization of standardized man."[123]) Now, since no other path is prac-ticable, the task is to intensify the process until it acquires another *dimension*, to reach the "zero point," the cape me-ridian, the equatorial point at which nihilism will brutally change its nature or night will disappear to make way for total light, when absolute destruction will be "alchemical-ly" transformed into absolute creation, thus proving once again that life is indestructible, that it contains a *secret kernel*, an invisible element of permanence at the heart of universal becoming, an ever-present generator of new forms in the heart of chaos. In *The Gordian Knot* (1953) Jünger will clarify this intuition once again:

> The hypothesis according to which nihilism will pass the line does not exclude the possibility of re-turning to the systems that preceded it. This about face is conceivable at the heart of its own models,

---

[123] Martin Heidegger, *Einführung in die Metaphysik* (1935), ed. Petra Jaeger (Frankfurt am Main: Klostermann, 1983), pp. 28–29; in English: *Introduction to Metaphysics*, 2nd ed., trans. Gregory Fried and Richard Polt (New Haven: Yale University Press, 2014), p. 41.

e.g., if one becomes conscious of the ambivalence of *zero*, which represents both non-being and the utterly different. Great surprises will then be possible, such as seeing nihilism reverse, revealing an unknown side of itself.

This position is particularly interesting, for we find in it once again all the elements of Jüngerian thought: the equivalence of contraries, the notion of a "perfection" equivalent to an *inversion*, to a radical tipping-over, "heroic realism" equivalent to "riding the tiger," and finally the idea that defeat can become a source of victory. Indirectly, Jünger rediscovers the state of mind that was his following the First World War; taking note of the desperate situation of Germany, as well as the vengefulness and hatred that had built up against it, he proclaimed, "Let me have my crime!" and wrote: "Perfect! Above all, no pity for us! This is a position we can work from. . . . For a long time now, we have been marching toward a *magical zero point*, that only he alone who possesses invisible reserves of strength will pass."

Heidegger's point of view is different. The use of quotation marks in the title of his essay ("Über 'die Linie'") by itself indicates a *shift* in the debate. The title chosen by Heidegger no longer means "past the line" (*trans lineam*) but "on the line," "regarding the line" (*de linea*). Seeking means of getting past nihilism, Jünger is assessing a *situation*. Heidegger instead proposes to identify "the *site* of the line that determines the source of nihilism's essence and of its fulfillment" (Granel, p. 200; cf. McNeill, p. 292). Only the identification of this "site" will allow us to understand what the fulfillment of nihilism consists of. By this notion of "fulfillment—distinct from realization (which is merely the cause of fulfillment)—we are to understand the "gathering of all elements essential to nihilism" (Granel, p. 209; cf. McNeill, p. 297). Fulfillment is not the *end*, but with it the final phase begins, that of the "zero line," which Heidegger confines himself to revealing in the distance: "The zero line, where fulfillment will reach its end, is not yet even slightly visible" (Granel, p. 210; cf. McNeill, p. 297).

For Jünger, once the height of nihilism has been reached, once the equator of destruction has been passed, things will clear up: "The moment when the line is crossed will reveal to us a new turning of Being; then that which really is will begin to reveal itself." Heidegger is skeptical. Is the real (i.e., that which is) truly going to begin to appear because Being will once more "turn" itself? Is it not rather the "new turning of Being that alone will reveal to us the favorable moment for crossing the line?" Is Being merely that which "turns itself toward men?" Does not the way Being "turns about and withdraws into absence" under the domination of nihilism constitute one of its "turnings"? And moreover, can Being and its "turning" even be dissociated? Heidegger concludes: "To speak of an turning of Being remains an accidental means, and one of the most problematic; for Being rests in the turning in such a way that the latter cannot ever simply come and add itself to Being" (Granel, p. 229; cf. McNeill, p. 308).

On the other hand, if it is true, as Jünger says, that man *undergoes* nihilism, it is just as certain that it was he who created it.

> If, in nihilism, non-being manages in a peculiar way to arrive at domination, then man is not merely struck with nihilism, but plays a substantial part in it. But in that case as well, all human "substance" does not remain somewhere on this side of the line, with the purpose of crossing it and establishing itself on the other side, close to Being. The Being of man itself belongs to the essence of nihilism, and similarly to the phase of fulfillment. (Granel, p. 233;

cf. McNeill, p. 311).

At last came the principal criticism, just as when in analyzing *The Worker* Heidegger reproaches Jünger in the end with remaining a faithful disciple of Nietzsche. He reproaches him with not abandoning the Nietzschean perspective, in his view *metaphysical*, of "value" and "Will to Power." The idea of an *overcoming* of nihilism, he observes, is clearly connected to Nietzsche: it involves the Will to Power as a means of realizing the overcoming. Now, according to Heidegger, the essence of nihilism, far from having the Will to Power as its antidote, *is fulfilled* in it. So, it is vain to oppose the Will to Power to nihilism, as the means best suited to triumphing over it, since the Will to Power is its cause:

> The movement toward ever less plenitude, ever less of the original within Being-as-a-whole, is not merely accompanied by an increase in the Will to Power but is even determined by it. . . . The reduction observed within Being rests on a production of Being, viz., on a development of the Will to Power as an unconditional will to will. (Granel, pp. 234–35; cf. McNeill, p. 312).

The idea of "crossing the line" is thus meaningless with respect to the goal being pursued, for it cannot lead to the zone of *fulfilled* nihilism: "The attempt to cross the line remains condemned to a representation that itself falls under the hegemony of the forgetting of Being. This is also why it expresses itself with the fundamental concepts of metaphysics: figure, value, transcendence" (Granel, p. 246; cf. McNeill, p. 319).

So, metaphysics remains the "homeland" of *Crossing the Line*, just as it was also the "homeland" of *The Worker*. Jünger, says Heidegger, intends to overcome nihilism, but his discourse remains metaphysical. The language of the metaphysics of the Will to Power, the language of figure and value, born of Western metaphysics and as such the fundamental source of contemporary nihilism, is preserved by Jünger, even once the "line" is crossed. It preserves "on the other side of the line the same sense as in *The Worker*, i.e., the sense of that which is *likened to the figure*" (Granel, p. 223; cf. McNeill, p. 305). Under these conditions, how can we speak of "overcoming"? Whence the fundamental question:

> Must the language of the Will to Power, the figure, value, be preserved on the other side of the critical line? What if the language, specifically, of metaphysics, and even that metaphysics itself (whether that of the living God or that of the death of God) constituted, *qua* metaphysics, that barrier that prevented the crossing of the line, i.e., the overcoming of nihilism? If this is so, should not the crossing of the line necessarily become a mutation of saying, and does it not demand a metamorphosis in the relation to the essence of language? (Granel, pp. 224–25; cf. McNeill, p. 306).

The procedure Heidegger proposes is different: "reflecting on the essence of nihilism, i.e., first of all taking the path that leads to situating the dwelling of Being." Now, "the question of Being perishes if it does not abandon the language of metaphysics, because metaphysical representation forbids thinking the question of the dwelling of Being" (Granel, p. 225; cf. McNeill, p. 306). So, everything finally depends on "right saying." If we do not manage to escape nihilism, it is because our language is not "yet capable of corresponding to the essence of Being" (Granel, p. 230; cf. McNeill, p. 309). In the final analysis, the essence of nihilism remains in metaphysics, i.e., in forgetfulness of Being; and, conversely, the "memory" of Being coincides with the completion of metaphysics. So, a true "overcoming" (*Überwindung*) of nihilism does not consist in "crossing the line" (that amounts only to *extending* nihilism). It consists in the "appropriation" (*Verwindung*) of metaphysics—in the appropriation of "this gathering in the essence that declares itself in the metaphysical thought of the West," and first of all in that decline (*Verfall*) into forgetfulness of Being that is nihilism's essential characteristic. To do this, "faithful thought" must clarify the essence of metaphysics. It must overcome metaphysics to *come back* to it in order to seize its reappropriated essence in its place, in its *dwelling*. This "appropriation" of metaphysics is obviously not a restoration. It is, on the contrary, the very condition that renders *impossible* any restoration of metaphysics insofar as it radically clarifies the question of nihilism in which the later resulted, and at the same time permits us to escape it. The extreme point of the outcome of metaphysics, nihilism unveils itself for what it is when the origin of that which produced it is also unveiled: "The place of the essence of accomplished nihilism . . . would be to seek where the essence of metaphysics develops its utmost possibilities and gathers itself in them" (Granel, p. 235; cf. McNeill, p. 313).

In the end, the question of overcoming nihilism resolves itself into the question "What is metaphysics?" posed by Heidegger in 1929, one year before the publication of *Total Mobilization*. In other words, to leave nihilism behind us—to leave it in that *place* that gives metaphysics its provenance—we must first enter into its essence: "Instead of wanting to overcome nihilism, we should try finally to enter, calmly and collectedly, into its essence" (Granel, p. 247; cf. McNeill, p. 319). Thus, we shall observe that the essence of nihilism is the "in-sane," but also, as such, an "indication towards the un-scathed." *In the most extreme danger grows that which saves.* Such a procedure involves meditating and giving proof of saying that indicates the domain of the essence of nihilism and the appropriation of metaphysics. There lies the greatest task to which we can dedicate a "faithful thought for the salvation of that which is given to us as destiny, and, in this destiny, as tradition" (Granel, p. 251; cf. McNeill, p. 321).

It is precisely to a meditation of the type to which Heidegger invited him that Jünger seems to have devoted himself his later years. On August 16, 1982, he told *Der Spiegel*: "My footbridge between the present and the future is meditation."[124] From *Subtle Hunts* to *Drugs and Intoxications*,[125] time passes. Arriving at the evening of his life, having himself passed the "meridian of nothingness," beloved especially by those who scarcely understood him, but often understood by those who did not like him, Ernst Jünger had nothing left to defend or condemn. Stricken year by year with the feeling of being, like Hyperion, a foreigner in his own country, and nevertheless having arrived

---

[124] Interview conducted by Rudolph Augstein, Hellmut Karasek, and Harald Wieser, published amid the polemics that developed in 1982 when Jünger was awarded the Goethe Prize of the City of Frankfurt. On these polemics, see especially Wolfgang Strauss, "Jüngers heroischer Existentialismus vom Blut, von der Wollust und vom Tode oder Kampf als inneres Erlebnis" ("Jünger's Heroic Existentialism of Blood, of Lust, and of Death or Struggle as an Inner Experience"), *Neue Zeit*, 1982, 5, pp. 15–22; and Karl Höffkes, "Die Negation der Schleife. Die politische konzeption des jungen Ernst Jünger" ("The Negation of the Loop: The Political Conception of the Young Ernst Jünger"), *Deutschland in Geschichte und Gegenwart*, 1983, 1, pp. 24–31. Before this, Jünger had in 1974 received the Schiller Prize of Baden-Würtemburg, and in 1977 the Golden Eagle of the Book Festival of Nice.

[125] Ernst Jünger, *Annährungen. Drogen und Rausch* (*Approaches: Drugs and Ecstasy*) (Stuttgart: Klett, 1970).

at the stage of honors, he could regard his work with a serene eye—the eye of an entomologist. At the end of his life, wrote Günther Barsch, he "returned in a certain way to Goethe as to his own origin." In fact, he had followed that "Goethean itinerary" illustrated by the expression: "When I am tired of seeking, I can discover that which I have found." He had gone from passion to detachment, from expressionism to the "romanticism of steel," then to the "heroic realism" of classicism. He had achieved objectivity concerning all his commitments. The principle of alternation, which Henry de Montherlant derived from a principle of equivalence, he had ended up overcoming, in the shadow of a sort of Western form of Shintoism—that religion he once said was "cut to his measure." Successively driven from one end of himself to another, he could henceforth realize the decisive synthesis, acceding to the stage of the Anarch, that sovereign figure who brings distance and power into harmony by dominating time.

This relation to time, which Jünger himself explored in *At the Wall of Time* (1959), evoking the image of the hourglass "waiting" for one to turn it over, has not always been well-understood. Very quickly, Jünger intuitively perceived the power of dominating and "abolishing" time that his brother Friedrich Georg had attributed to the god Pan. Moreover, one finds terms such as "modern" and "modernity" only occasionally in his works; they clearly do not have much meaning for him. Like Heidegger in his forest hut, he has "made the *untimely* choice of rural life at Kirchhorst or Wilflingen, in houses surrounded by gardens where he does not fear to do the work of a gardener."[126] At the end of *The Gordian Knot*, he writes:

Return is inconceivable without an immobile

---

[126] Julien Hervier, "Ernst Jünger et la question de modernité" ("Ernst Jünger and the Question of Modernity"), *Revue d'Allemagne*, XIV, 1, January–March 1982.

center. . . . If we assume an intimate, immobile, atemporal, and unextended essence at the center of becoming, as in the hub of a wheel, we can also admit that the constellations meet in it, for example, before and after, you and me, East and West. . . . At bottom, there is only *one* return. It occurs when man recognizes the emergence of the eternal within time. The world then becomes dense. That way of knowing which is remembrance, or veneration, is an aspect of this. It is the part man takes in reality. It cannot be without him.

Ever the coincidence of contraries—behold the memory of a very ancient cosmogony . . .

In *Eumeswil*, the character of the Anarch is the perfect incarnation of this "immobile center." Within the work of Jünger, *Eumeswil* is to be situated along the line of the great "utopian novels" that already include *Heliopolis*. The two works are, however, very different. Jünger himself will say:

Heliopolis is situated upon a really lived historical experience, while *Eumeswil* describes something that exists at far deeper levels. These two books are, if you will, successive steps of a development that can be thought of not as rectilinear, but like the growth of a bamboo shoot, knot after knot, or according to the principle of the spiral mentioned by Goethe: you think you have arrived back at your point of departure, but you are in reality at a higher level.[127]

Eumeswil is, besides, a book in which Jünger once again creates a figure—the third, after the Worker and the Re-

---

[127] Interview with Jean-Louis de Rambures in *Le Monde*.

bel—and this is enough to make clear that the book occupies a central place within his works. More than ever,
Jünger does here the work of a prophet. The universe he
stages is a universe *not yet born*, whose terminal phase he
still manages to discern. The "Mauritanian" society
reigned over by Condor, the tyrant with an artist's sensi-
bility, and his chief-of-staff, the icy Domo, follows the realization of the world state. The latter is so overextended
that it is in process of disintegration. *Power* here is once
again at the heart of things: "At the front of the stage, the
game of Power is celebrated; to the rear, behind the
scenes, the powers behind power unveil themselves" (Armin Mohler). The Anarch, a character gifted with an extraordinary power of adaptation, and who occupies the
entire foreground, is not, like the Rebel, a simple adversary of that power which Jünger once made the domain of
the Worker. He incarnates *another form* of it. He is "not
the adversary of the monarch, but rather his pendant"—
and it is in this respect, it seems, that he represents a *synthesis* of the Worker and the Rebel. The Anarch is an actor
precisely insofar as he renounces being an actor, insofar as
he apparently wants to be a "spectator," the better to understand the course of things. This is how he is perfectly
sovereign. If you prefer, the Anarch is at the center of the
universe, not by "localization" but by vocation: he *institutes the center wherever he is*. He is the hub of the wheel
which turns and sets all things in motion; he is in the eye
of the cyclone. So, we find once again the Olympian attitude: the absolute of time abolishes time and dominates
it. But we also find once again an idea constantly present
in Jünger: that of an element of permanence nested within
the very heart of that which becomes. During the First
World War, the intensification of the mobility of the armies resulted in the war of position, in the immobility of
the soldiers in the trenches. The dazzling progress of
technology issued in an immobile "point of perfection."

And in *The Worker* we already read:

> The more we dedicate ourselves to speed, the more intimately we should be persuaded that it disguises a being at rest, and that every acceleration is merely the translation of an imperishable native language.

Order installs itself in the midst of chaos where "being at rest" is hiding. Günther Barsh was not wrong to say: "Ernst Jünger is a natural phenomenon which escapes all ordered schemata to establish his own order."[128]

On careful examination, and beyond all that separates them, every one of the figures created by Jünger are "immobile centers" in the midst of becoming. The Worker is the figure that gives the age its fixed form. The Rebel maintains in the face of technology's power the very possibility of conserving that which is truly important. The Anarch institutes the center by his mere presence. And it is the same concern for a positive *freedom* that motivates the appearance of these three faces. In this respect we can imagine a quasi-Hegelian schema where the "thesis" of the Worker is opposed to the "antithesis" of the Rebel before resulting in the "synthesis" of the Anarch. Let us not forget that the will to make contraries coincide—to cause them to fuse to give form to a new, superior element—is at the very heart of Jünger's procedure. Jünger wrote to Henri Placard on the subject of North and South (September 24, 1978):

> My passion, in this domain as in many others, is ambivalent—between Verdi, whose monument I visit on all my trips to Cagliari, and *The Phantom Ship*. The North Sea in its nocturnal tempests, the Mediterranean at high noon—Wagner and Nie-

---

[128] *Criticón*, March–April 1975, p. 48.

tzsche reunited.

In his foreword to the new translation of *Storm of Steel* published by Plon in 1960 there occurs this remarkable sentence: "The potter, with his *two* hands, gives a form to the clay as it turns. Similarly, the two adversaries modeled the face of the future." Jünger is speaking, of course, of the two sides that confronted one another during the Great War; it was thanks to their *conjoined* efforts that the future *took form*. But the scope of the statement is broader. Contraries must struggle with one another in order to produce. The *new* does not arise in the world, does not take form in the world, except under the action of antagonistic forces, in such a way that these forces, opposed to one another though they may be, are at the same time *allies* in giving birth to that which succeeds them. (We find here a whole polemological view of life, in which the adversary can never, by nature, be an *absolute enemy*, but only a figure of adversity for the moment, complementary in the end to that which is opposed to him.) Similarly, nothing forbids us from thinking that the immobile figure in the midst of becoming can also metamorphose into the *only mobile element* in an entirely fixed landscape.

It is in terms of this coincidence of contraries, and the conception of time that is unveiled therein, that we must consider Jünger's work and its apparent "contradictions." We then perceive that these "contradictions" are in fact points of view that, starting from opposed points, *converge* in order to respond to the same questioning and are arranged about a single procedure. The "disconnection" between the Jünger of youth and of maturity is in reality altogether relative, like all disconnections of this sort. Where there is a break there is also continuity. Similarly, we better understand whence comes the "timeliness" of Jünger's writing. It comes from an always *untimely* aim. *The Worker* is a striking example. This work, which seemed to so many observers as the most closely tied of all Jünger's works to a given political and historical situation, is perhaps that which is most distant from any—and it is precisely from this that it draws its *permanent timeliness*. If Jünger, in other words, was able to identify with such cold lucidity the dominant figure of our age,[129] this is above all because he was able to achieve the necessary *distance* from it. *The Worker* "is not a political work," Jünger confirmed to Daniel Rondeau.[130] It is in fact much more than that. It is untimely, and thereby *always* timely; and, conversely, Jünger's novels and essays that are the most visibly "distant" from the present moment always in fact relate to it in some essential way. In the conception of history implicitly posited by Jünger, the "past" by the same title as the "future" are *always there*, given in all timeliness. The age of the Worker continues today, like that of the "Great Woodsman." "Far from belonging to the historical context of Germany in 1933," observes Jean-Michel Palmier, "*The Worker* appears as a star that shines before us, in the future." In this book which to the highest degree marks the "past" of its author lies also the secret of our "future." Jünger said so himself: *The Worker* is "behind" him—but "ahead" of us.

For the moment, we are in the interregnum, the *Zwischenreich*. To Jacques Le Rider, Jünger declared: "This age is only a transition."[131] To Nicole Casanova: "We are in the period when the old values are dead and the new are not yet in action."[132] Still plunged in that "World Civil War" whose preliminaries Jünger had seen emerge before

---

[129] Concerning Jünger, Julien Hervier writes: "His merit as a revolutionary conservative is to have always refused to close his eyes to the present, whose characteristic elements he has better identified than many progressive writers" (op. cit., p. 147).

[130] *Libération*, January 16, 1983.

[131] *Le Monde-Dimanche*, August 29, 1982.

[132] *Les Nouvelles littéraire*, October 13, 1977.

his eyes, we are living in a society in crisis, no longer productive of culture. We are in Alexandria in the time of the
Diadokhoi, "with all those museums, those great lexica,
that *chinoiserie* of intellectuals." We are at the "midnight
of history," and our age more than ever resembles that
"mixture of museum and construction site" evoked in *The
Worker*. This idea of "interregnum" which Jünger often
spoke about during his last years has its origins in Nietzsche's thought and constitutes one of the key themes of
the Conservative Revolution. But Jünger, as usual, gives it
a significance that transcends politics to reach metaphysics and the "cosmic." It is no longer simply a question of
an "old order" that we might vainly wish to restore, nor of
a "new order" yet to be born, but of a more fundamental
caesura: "We find ourselves at the turning point between
two ages whose importance corresponds almost to the
passage from the stone age to the age of metals."

It is during the interregnum that the titans are unleashed; but there is no one is left to restrain them. During
the interregnum, technology triumphs. The bourgeois as
well. Today, Jünger could no longer write: "If we consider
a century of German history, we can observe with pride
that we have been bad *bourgeois*" (p. 11). But what exactly
is the relation between technology and the bourgeois?
Both are "products" of rationalizing and calculating
thought: the emergence of technology goes hand in hand
with the rise of egalitarian rationality born and spread by
bourgeois values. But is this enough for us to say that
nothing separates them? Does there not exist, at the heart
of technology, in regard to the bourgeois type, a deep contradiction between the strengthening of the means of
power that characterizes its development, and the irenic,
antipolemological character of a bourgeois ideology that
increasingly turns upon the hedonist ideal of self-
domestication and individual material "happiness"? The
development of technology seems to create the latent

"temptation" to use the new means of power at the very moment when the ideology involved in the emergence of these new powers *also* generates the inhibition of having recourse to them. The same ideology and the same type thus give birth both to the challenge and to that which forbids the challenge to be met *on its own level*, in order to prevent technology from instituting itself as its own end. In *The Worker*, Jünger said: "To maintain a real relation with technology, one must be more than a technician" (p. 149). But where today is this "more?" Does the reign of technology suffer merely from an "absence of *more*"—or, more radically, should we consider that technology is precisely *that which ineluctably realizes the annihilation of a "more"*? To say that technology sets itself up as a master because no one wants to be *its* master may at first glance appear seductive. But in reality, is not technology that which by nature prevents the birth of a "master"?

After the war, opposing the fury of technology, Jünger first of all created a figure of resistance. The Rebel is the man who adopts an almost physical distance in order to preserve, apart, the chances for freedom. The figure of the Anarch succeeded it. The distance became mental and spiritual; it is no longer antagonistic to power, but another, more sovereign power develops *above and beyond* it. Nevertheless, the fundamental problem has still been posed. Is the Anarch merely the man who "pulls his own chestnuts out of the fire" at the point where technology has reached (and passed) its "point of perfection"? Is he the *last figure*, or could one envision another figure who would be capable of using technology no longer in the service of the elemental forces of destruction, but to struggle *against* those forces of destruction? Is such a perspective compatible with what we know of the *essence* of technology? The essence of technology does not belong to technology, but to that which *founds* it. As Jean-Michel Palmier has observed, it is not the industrial development

of modern times that made our age the "era of technology," but "it is because the historic fundament of the present age makes possible—accomplishes itself—in technology that we live today in the era of technology." Now,
to "think" the essence of technology, we must think of
something besides technology. Heidegger demonstrated
this: just as for the essence of nihilism, it is only by starting from the essence of metaphysics that the essence of
modern technology can be understood. It is thus confirmed that the essence of technology is not neutral, and
this is what explains how, left to itself, technology obeys
its essence, *reveals* its essence by exercising a destructive
action upon the world. But if technology, precisely in its
essence, is not neutral, how can one expect to dominate
it? How can the man who *inhabits* the essence of technology hope to make it his "instrument" in a positive sense?

However, if it is true that contraries are always destined to meet, if it is true that by returning to the essence
of nihilism, one escapes nihilism, just as by returning to
the essence of metaphysics one puts an end to the decline
of Being into forgetfulness, should one not also envisage
returning to the essence of technology? Heidegger often
quoted the verse of Hölderlin: "Where the danger is, there
grows that which saves" ("Patmos"). The same goes for
deserts: they form "a space from whence man can maintain hope, fight his fight, and even triumph." Technology
then reveals itself in all its ambivalence. It is the most
fearful of dangers, since it masks the domain of openness
to truth, but at the same time it is "*a kind of unveiling . . .
i.e., of truth.*"[133] Supreme peril and perhaps the last plank
of salvation, it expresses the most total forgetting of the
question of Being (*Seinsfrage*), but it is at the same time
the current mode in which Being reveals itself to us. It is
that mode of dissimulation and unveiling of which

---

[133] Martin Heidegger, "Die Frage nach der Technik," op. cit.

Heidegger says that it must be understood as pro-vocation (*Heraus-Forderung*) and as framework (*Gestell*).

To escape the nihilism produced by forgetfulness of Being is to *go back* to "reappropriate" the essence of nihilism, the essence of metaphysics, the essence of technology. It is to find the conditions for a *new beginning*, placing man in a different relation to the world from the one established by two millennia of Western metaphysics. But is man capable of such an effort? Is he capable of it *by himself*? The great problem that Jünger never ceased to confront is *meaning*. The question he was asking himself at the end of the First World War was, how can one give *meaning* to the sacrifice of the dead soldiers? In *The Worker*, the creation of forms made possible by technology was supposed to give birth to a new order equivalent to a new *significance*. Today, in view of the fury of technology, the problem remains: how can one give meaning back to the life of man?

Western metaphysics, which is also arriving today at its "point of perfection," has involved the death—or departure—of the gods. It is also for this reason that it ended in nihilism and the fury of elementary, titanic forces: *the death of the gods leaves the field open for the titans*. In the past, such a situation already occurred, and the danger represented by the titans was overcome. The gods mastered the titans. They enchained Prometheus. And the way they waged that war against the titans tells us how they might also wage it in the future. *Myth*, in describing this struggle against a titanic element ever ready to be reborn, ever ready to profit from the breakdown of the *alliance between gods and men*, once again *speaks* to us. It tells us what will happen, if we want it. The reign of technology will end in the most extreme distress. The gods will again have to go to battle with the titans in order to put an end to chaos. The fall of the titans will come. The interregnum will end. Another beginning will occur.

What can one do to hasten the return of the gods? In ancient times, men created gods, just as gods created men. Gods went *to meet men*, for the latter were in such a state of mind and held to such a conception of the world that this "encounter" was possible. Men and gods are thus in a relation of *mutual creation*, of mutual dependence. Each is the *condition* of the other. For Heidegger, to be a *poet* in a time of distress is to be *attentive to the vestiges of the gods who have fled and to the call of the gods to come.* And he also cites Hölderlin's words: "That which remains, the poets establish," which Jünger takes up again in *The Gordian Knot.* Indeed, only the poetic attitude can perceive the presence of a divine force underlying the chaos.

Tempted for a time after the last war by certain aspects of Christian thought, Jünger later evoked the gods ever more insistently. He observes that the ancient gods have left: "the gods will never pass our way again." Regarding the future, he declares:

> Two outcomes are possible: either the Ant Heap State described by Huxley, or things will happen which have little to do with politics, but rather with theology or theophany. The gods themselves will make their appearance. This was the opinion of, among others, Hölderlin, Nietzsche, and, closer to our own time, Heidegger. As concerns myself, I hold to strict neutrality. Or rather, I would say, *cum grano salis*, that I prefer to observe the course of things. For now, let us allow the gods to show themselves. I do not at all consider this an impossibility: the more history contracts, the more it leaves the field open for extrahistorical events. After which there will be plenty of time to deliberate.

To Jean Plumyène in 1977 he said:

Nietzsche and Heidegger await the appearance of the gods. From the point where we are, it is going to be necessary to advance toward the gods. It is true that something will have to come from the Other Side. The gods will have to approach us. As when one builds a bridge . . .

To which he adds:

Biologists are engaging in manipulations, creating new aptitudes. Others want to return to divine things. These technicians are new titans. Soon they are going to meet the gods. No one knows what will happen then.

Three years later, he confided to Gilles Lapouge:

Man's solitude is increasing, the desert is spreading around us, but perhaps it is in the desert that the gods will come. . . . The ancient gods, I agree with Nietzsche, are dead. But the gods are necessary, and we must go to meet them.[134]

Jünger thinks that the Age of Aquarius we are now entering will be characterized by intense spiritualization. But the entrance to this age passes through a brutal, elemental, and titanic phase: "I have great hopes, but not in our current time." The present situation is tragic. On the one hand, man cannot escape destiny, or elude the "technological" process now underway; on the other hand, he cannot, in order to dominate this process, have recourse to any known formula. Ancient values are of no further help. Accompanied by Dionysius and Apollo, will Pan once again assert himself as the god of "wild profusion?"

---

[134] *La Quinzaine Littéraire*, February 16, 1980.

Ernst Jünger reserves his response and keeps his secret: between "alchemy" and entomology, he leaves us a "work in black." The end of the reign of the titans demands a revolution, which will not necessarily be a revolution of men. It will be, rather, a *revolution of the Earth itself.* But the titans are sons of the earth as well. On September 24, 1978, Jünger writes again to Henri Plard:

> The Worker is a titan, and as such, a son of the Earth; he follows, as Nietzsche says, the direction of the Earth, to the very point where he seems to destroy it. Vulcanism will intensify. The Earth will not only cause new genuses to arise, but also new orders. As for the Overman, he still belongs to the species. . . . To start with, the overthrow of the gods—the material assault against the paternalistic world with its principles, its priests, and its heroes—has not yet ended. The reply will live up to the attack. Hesiod and the Edda will become timely.

Soldier, Worker, Rebel, Anarch:
Types & Figures in Jünger's Writings[*]

In Jünger's writings, four great figures appear successively, each corresponding to a quite distinct period of the
author's life. They are, chronologically, the Front Soldier,
the Worker, the Rebel, and the Anarch. Through these
figures one can divine the passionate interest Jünger has
always had for the world of forms. Forms, for him, cannot
result from chance occurrences in the sensible world. Rather, forms guide, on various levels, the ways sensible beings express themselves: the history of the world is above
all morphogenesis. As an entomologist, moreover, Jünger
was naturally inclined to classifications. Beyond the individual, he identifies the species or the kind. One can see
here a subtle sort of challenge to individualism: "The
unique and the typical exclude one another," he writes.
Thus, as Jünger sees it, the universe is one in which figures
give epochs their metaphysical significance. In this brief
exposition, I will compare and contrast the great figures
identified by Jünger.

* * *

The Front Soldier (*Frontsoldat*) is, first of all, witness
to the end of classical wars: wars that gave priority to the
chivalrous gesture, that were organized around the concepts of glory and honor, that generally spared civilians,
and that distinguished clearly between the front and the
rear. "Though once we crouched in bomb craters, we still

---

[*] "Types et figures dans l'oeuvre d'Ernst Jünger: Le Soldat du
front, le Travailleur, le Rebelle et l'Anarque," was originally presented as a lecture in Rome in May 1997.

believed," Jünger wrote, "that man was stronger than *matériel*. That proved to be an error." Indeed, from then on, the "material" counted more than the human factor. This material factor signifies the irruption and dominion of technology. Technology imposes its own law, the law of impersonality and total war—a war simultaneously massive and abstract in its cruelty. At the same time, the Soldier becomes an impersonal actor. His very heroism is impersonal, because what counts most for him is no longer the goal or outcome of combat. It is not win or lose, live or die. What counts is the spiritual disposition that leads him to accept his anonymous sacrifice. In this sense, the Front Soldier is by definition an unknown soldier, who forms a body, in all senses of the term, with the unit to which he belongs, like a tree which is not only a part of the forest but an exemplary incarnation of it.

The same applies to the Worker, who appears in 1932, in the famous book of the same name, the subtitle of which is "Dominion and Form."[1] The common element of the Soldier and Worker is active impersonality. They are both children of technology, because the same technology that transformed war into monotonous "work," drowning the chivalrous spirit in the mud of the trenches, has also transformed the world into a vast workshop in which man is henceforth completely enthralled[2] by the imperatives of

---

[1] Ernst Jünger, *Der Arbeiter: Herrschaft und Gestalt* (*The Worker: Dominion and Form*) (Hamburg: Hanseatische Verlagsanstalt, 1932).

[2] The French is *"arraisonne."* Here the verb *arraisonner* has the sense of "to enthrall," with the dual sense of "to capture" and "to captivate." Later in this essay, Benoist uses *"arraisonnement"* as equivalent to Heidegger's *"Gestell"* or *"Ge-stell,"* which is usually translated into English as "enframing." According to Heidegger, *Gestell* is the view of the world as a stockpile (*Bestand*) of resources for human manipulation. Heidegger calls *Gestell* the "essence" of technology, because it is the worldview

productivity. Soldier and Worker, finally, have the same enemy: the contemptible bourgeois liberal, the "last man" announced by Nietzsche, who venerates moral order, utility, and profit. Also, the Worker and the Soldier returned from the front both want to destroy in order to create, to give up the last shreds of individualism in order to found a new world on the ruins of the old "petrified form of life."

However, while the Soldier was only the passive subject of the reign of technology, the Worker aims actively to identify himself with it. Far from being its subject, or submitting to its manifestations, the Worker, on the contrary, seeks in all conscience to affirm the power of technology that he thinks will abolish the differences between the classes, as well as between peace and war, civilian and Soldier. The Worker is no longer one who is "sacrificed to carry the burdens in the great deserts of fire," as Jünger still put it in the *The Forest Path*,[3] but a being entirely devoted to "total mobilization."[4] Thus the figure of the Worker goes far beyond the type of the Front Soldier. For the Worker—who dreams all the while of a Spartan, Prussian, or Bolshevik life, where the individual would be definitively outclassed by the type—the Great War was only the anvil at which was forged another way of being in the world. The Front Soldier limited himself in order to embody new norms of collective existence. The Worker, for

---

that makes modern technological civilization possible. See Martin Heidegger, "The Question concerning Technology," trans. William Lovitt, in Martin Heidegger, *Basic Writings*, ed. David Farrell Krell, 2nd ed. (New York: Harper, 1993)—Ed.

[3] Ernst Jünger, *Der Waldgang* (*The Forest Path*) (Frankfurt am Main: Vittorio Klostermann, 1951)—Ed.

[4] Ernst Jünger, *Die totale Mobilmachung* (Berlin: Verlag der Zeitkritik, 1931); English translation: "Total Mobilization," trans. Joel Golb and Richard Wolin, in Richard Wolin, ed., *The Heidegger Controversy: A Critical Reader* (New York: Columbia University Press, 1991)—Ed.

his part, intends to transplant them into civilian life, to make them the law of the whole society.

The Worker is thus not merely the man who works (the most common meaning), any more than he is the man of a social class, i.e., of a given economic category (the historical meaning). He is the Worker in a metaphysical sense: the one who reveals work as the general law of a world that devotes itself entirely to efficiency and productivity, even in leisure and rest.

The elements of Jünger's worldview are sometimes summarized with the phrase "heroic realism." This includes his aesthetic and voluntarist conception of technology, his decisionism of every moment, the opposition of the Worker to the bourgeois, and the Nietzschean will "to transvalue all values" which already underlay Jünger's "soldierly nationalism" of the twenties. However, under the influence of events, Jünger's thinking would soon undergo a decisive inflection, which took it in another direction entirely.

The turn corresponds to the novel *On the Marble Cliffs*,[5] published in 1939. The heroes of the story, two brothers, herbalists from the Great Marina who recoil in horror at the inexorable outcome of the Great Woodsman's enterprise, discover that there are weapons stronger than those that pierce and kill. Jünger, at that time, was not only informed by the rise of Nazism, he was influenced by his brother, Friedrich Georg Jünger, who in a famous book[6] was one of the first to work out a radical

---

[5] Ernst Jünger, *Auf den Marmorklippen* (Hamburg: Hanseatische Verlagsanstalt, 1939); English translation: *On the Marble Cliffs: A Novel*, trans. Stuart Hood (London: John Lehman, 1947).

[6] Friedrich Georg Jünger, *Die Perfektion der Technik* (*The Perfection of Technology*) (Frankfurt am Main: Klostermann, 1946); English translation: *The Failure of Technology: Perfection without Purpose*, trans. F. D. Wieck (Hinsdale, Ill.: Henry Regnery,

critique of the technological framework.[7] As children of technology, the Soldier and especially the Worker were on the side of the titans. Yet Ernst Jünger came to see that the titanic reign of the elemental leads straight to nihilism. He understood that the world should be neither interpreted nor changed but viewed as the very source of the unveiling of truth (*aletheia*). He understood that technology is not necessarily antagonistic to bourgeois values, and that it transforms the world only by globalizing the desert. He understood that, behind history, timelessness returns to more essential categories, and that human time, marked by the wheels of the watch, is an "imaginary time," founded on an artifice that made men forgetful of their belonging to the world, a time that fixes the nature of their projects instead of the reverse, unlike the hourglass, the "elementary clock" whose flow obeys natural laws—a cyclic not a linear time. Jünger, in other words, realized that the outburst of the titans is first and foremost a revolt against the gods. This is why he dismissed Prometheus. The collective figures were succeeded by personal ones.

Against totalitarian despotism, the heroes of *On the Marble Cliffs* choose withdrawal, taking a distance. By this, they already announce the attitude of the Rebel, of whom Jünger would write: "The Rebel is . . . whoever the law of his nature puts in relation to freedom, a relation that in time brings him to a revolt against automatism and a refusal to accept its ethical consequence, fatalism."

The figure of the Rebel is thus directly connected to a meditation on freedom—and also on exclusion, since the Rebel is equally an outlaw. The Rebel is still a combatant, like the Front Soldier, but he is a combatant who repudiates active impersonality, because he intends to preserve his freedom with respect to the cause he defends. In this

---

1949).

[7] *"l'arraisonnement technicien"*—Ed.

sense, the Rebel cannot be identified with one system or another, even the one for which he fights. He is not at ease in any them. If the Rebel chooses marginalization, it is above all to guard against the forces of destruction, to break the encirclement, one might say, using a military metaphor that Jünger himself employs when he writes, "The incredible encirclement of man was prepared long ago by the theories that aim at giving a flawless logical explanation of the world and that march in lockstep with the development of technology."

"The mysterious way goes towards the interior," said Novalis. The Rebel is an emigrant to the interior, who seeks to preserve his freedom in the heart of the forests where "paths that go nowhere" intersect. This refuge, however, is ambiguous, because this sanctuary of organic life not yet absorbed by the mechanization of the world represents—to the precise extent that it constitutes a universe foreign to human norms—the "great house of death, the very seat of the destructive danger." Hence the position of the Rebel can only be provisional.

The last figure, whom Jünger calls the Anarch, first appeared in 1977 in *Eumeswil*,[8] a "postmodern" novel intended as a sequel to *Heliopolis*[9] and set in the third millennium. Venator, the hero, no longer needs to resort to the forest to remain untouched by the ambient nihilism. It is enough for him to have reached an elevation that allows him to observe everything from a distance without needing to move away. Typical in this respect is his attitude toward power. Whereas the Anarchist wants to abolish power, the Anarch is content to break all ties to it. The

---

[8] Ernst Jünger, *Eumeswil* (Stuttgart: Klett-Cotta, 1977); English translation: *Eumeswil*, trans. Joachim Neugroschel (New York: Marsilio, 1993).

[9] Ernst Jünger, *Heliopolis: Rückblick auf eine Stadt* (*Heliopolis: Review of a City*) (Tübingen: Heliopolis, 1949)—Ed.

Anarch is not the enemy of power or authority, but he does not seek them, because he does not need them to become who he is. The Anarch is sovereign of himself—which amounts to saying that he shows the distance that exists between sovereignty, which does not require power, and power, which never confers sovereignty. "The Anarch," Jünger writes, "is not the partner of the monarch, but his antipode, the man that power cannot grasp and who is also a danger to it. He is not the adversary of the monarch, but his opposite." A true chameleon, the Anarch adapts to all things, because nothing reaches him. He is in service of history while being beyond it. He lives in all times at once, present, past, and future. Having crossed "the wall of time," he is in the position of the pole star, which remains fixed while the whole starry vault turns around it, the central axis or hub, the "center of the wheel where time is abolished." Thus, he can watch over the "clearing" which represents the place and occasion for the return of the gods. From this, one can see, as Claude Lavaud writes regarding Heidegger, that salvation lies "in hanging back, rather than crossing over; in contemplation, not in calculation; in the commemorative piety that opens thought to the revealing and concealing that together are the essence of *aletheia*."[10]

What distinguishes the Rebel from the Anarch is thus the quality of their voluntary marginalization: horizontal withdrawal for the former, vertical withdrawal for the latter. The Rebel needs to take refuge in the forest, because he is a man without power or sovereignty, and because it is only there that he retains the conditions of his freedom. The Anarch himself is also without power, but it is precisely because he is without power that he is sovereign.

---

[10] "'Über die Linie': Penser l'être dans l'ombre du nihilisme" ("'Over the Line': Thinking of Being in the Shadow of Nihilism"), *Les Carnets Ernst Jünger* 1 (1996), p. 49.

The Rebel is still in revolt, while the Anarch is beyond re-volt. The Rebel carries on in secret—he hides in the shad-ows—while the Anarch remains in plain sight. Finally, whereas the Rebel is banished by society, the Anarch ban-ishes himself. He is not excluded; he is emancipated.

* * *

The advent of the Rebel and Anarch relegated the memory of the Front Soldier to the background, but it did not end the reign of the Worker. Admittedly, Jünger changed his opinion of what we should expect, but the conviction that this figure really dominates today's world was never abandoned. The Worker, defined as the "chief titan who traverses the scene of our time," is really the son of the Earth, the child of Prometheus. He incarnates this "telluric" power of which modern technology is the in-strument. He is also a metaphysical figure, because mod-ern technology is nothing other than the realized essence of a metaphysics that sets man up as the master of a world transformed into an object. And with man, the Worker maintains a dialectic of possession: the Worker possesses man to the very extent that man believes he possesses the world by identifying himself with the Worker.

However, to the precise extent that they are the repre-sentatives of the elementary and telluric powers, the titans continue to carry a message whose meaning orders our existence. Jünger no longer regards them as allies, but nei-ther does he regard them as enemies. As is his habit, Jünger is a seismograph: he has a presentiment that the reign of the titans announces the return of the gods, and that nihilism is a necessary part of the passage towards the regeneration of the world. To finish with nihilism, we must live it to its end—"passing the line" which corre-sponds to the "meridian zero"—because, as Heidegger says, the technological framework[11] (*Ge-stell*) is still a mode of Being, not merely a mode of Being's oblivion. This is why, if Jünger sees the Worker as a danger, he also says that this danger can be our salvation, because it is by and through the Worker that it will be possible to *exhaust* the danger.

* * *

It is easy to see what differentiates the two couples formed, on the one hand, by the Front Soldier and the Worker, and, on the other, by the Rebel and the Anarch. But one would be wrong to conclude from this that the "second Jünger" of *On the Marble Cliffs* is the antithesis of the first. Rather, this "second Jünger" actually represents a development of an inclination present from the beginning but obscured by the work of the writer-soldier and the nationalist polemicist. In Jünger's first books, as well as in *Battle as Inner Experience* [12] and *Storm*,[13] one actually sees, between the lines of the narrative, an undeniable tendency toward the *vita contemplativa*. From the beginning, Jünger expresses a yearning for meditative reflection that descriptions of combat or calls to action cannot mask. This yearning is particularly evident in the first version of *The Adventurous Heart*,[14] where one can read not only a concern for a certain literary poetry, but also a reflection that could be described as both mineral and crystalline. It is a reflection on the immutability of things and on that

---

[11] *"l'arraisonnement"*—Ed.

[12] Ernst Jünger, *Der Kampf als inneres Erlebnis* (*Battle as Inner Experience*) (Berlin: Mittler, 1922)—Ed.

[13] Ernst Jünger, *Sturm* (written 1923) (Stuttgart: Ernst Klett, 1978)—Ed.

[14] Ernst Jünger, *Das Abenteuerliche Herz: Aufzeichnungen bei Tag und Nacht* (*The Adventurous Heart: Sketches by Day and Night*) (Berlin: Frundsberg, 1929).

which, in the very heart of the present, raises us up to cosmic signs and a recognition of the infinite, thus nurturing the "stereoscopic vision" in which two flat images merge to reveal the dimension of depth.

There is thus no contradiction between the four figures, but only a progressive deepening, a kind of increasingly fine sketch that led Jünger, initially an actor in his time, to then place himself finally above his time, as judge and critic, in order to testify to what came before his time and what will come after.

Already in *The Worker* one reads: "The more we dedicate ourselves to change, the more we must be intimately persuaded that behind it hides a calm being." Throughout his life, Jünger never ceased approaching this "calm being." While passing from manifest action to apparent non-action—while going, one might say, from beings to Being—he achieved an existential progression that finally allowed him to occupy the place of the Anarch, the unmoving center, the "central point of the turning wheel" from which all movement proceeds.

APPENDIX: ON TYPE & FIGURE [15]

In 1963, in his book entitled *Type—Name—Figure*,[16] Jünger writes: "Figure and type are higher forms of vision. The conception of figures confers a metaphysical power, the apprehension of types an intellectual power." We will reconsider this distinction between figure and type. But let us note immediately that Jünger connects the ability to distinguish them with a higher form of vision, i.e., with a

---

[15] The following Appendix is section one of the original lecture, followed by the last paragraph of section three. I have grouped them here for ease of reading—Ed.

[16] Ernst Jünger, *Typus—Name—Gestalt* (Stuttgart: Ernst Klett, 1963).

vision that goes beyond immediate appearances to seek
and identify archetypes. Moreover, he implies that this
higher form of vision merges with its object, i.e., with the
figure and the type. Furthermore, he specifies: "The type
does not appear in nature, or the figure in the universe.
Both must be deciphered in the phenomena, like a force
in its effects or a text in its characters." Finally, he affirms
that there exists a "typifying power of the universe," which
"seeks to pierce through the undifferentiated," and which
"acts directly on vision," causing an "ineffable knowledge:
intuition," then conferring a name: "The things do not
bear a name, names are conferred upon them."

This concern with transcending immediate appearances should not be misinterpreted. Jünger does not offer
us a new version of the Platonic allegory of the cave. He
does not suggest seeking the traces of another world in
this world. On the contrary, in *The Worker*, he already
denounced "the dualism of the world and its systems."
Likewise, in his *Paris Diaries*,[17] he wrote: "The visible contains all the signs that lead to the invisible. And the existence of the latter must be demonstrable in the visible
model." Thus, for Jünger, there is transcendence only in
immanence. And when he intends to seek the "things that
are behind things," to use the expression he employs in his
"Letter to the Man in the Moon," it is while being convinced, like Novalis, that "the real is just as magical as the
magical is real."[18]

One would also err gravely by comparing the type to a
"concept" and the figure to an "idea." "A type," Jünger

---

[17] In Ernst Jünger, *Strahlungen* (*Emanations*) (Tübingen:
Heliopolis, 1949).

[18] Ernst Jünger, "Sizilischer Brief an den Mann im Mond"
("Sicilian Letter to the Man in the Moon"), in *Blätter und Steine*
(*Leaves and Stones*) (Hamburg: Hanseatische Verlagsanstalt,
1934).

writes, "is always stronger than an idea, even more so than a concept." Indeed, the type is apprehended by vision, i.e., as image, whereas the concept can be grasped only by thought. Thus to apprehend the figure or the type is not to leave the sensible world for some other world that constitutes its first cause, but to seek in the sensible world the invisible dimension that constitutes the "typifying power": "We recognize individuals: the type acts as the matrix of our vision. . . . That really shows that it is not so much the type that we perceive but, in it and behind it, the power of the typifying source."

The German word for figure is *Gestalt*, which one generally translates as "form."[19] The nuance is not unimportant, because it confirms that the figure is anchored in the world of forms, i.e., in the sensible world, instead of being a Platonic idea, which would find in this world only its mediocre and deformed reflection. Goethe, in his time, was dismayed to learn that Schiller thought that his Ur-Plant (*Urpflanze*, archetypal plant) was an idea. The figure is often misunderstood in the very same way, as Jünger himself emphasized. The figure is on the side of vision as it is on the side of Being, which is consubstantial with the world. It is not on the side of *verum*, but of *certum*.

Let us now see what distinguishes the figure and the type. Compared to the figure, which is more inclusive but also fuzzier, the type is more limited. Its contours are rela-

---

[19] The first volume of Oswald Spengler's *Decline of the West* (1916) already bore the subtitle: *Gestalt und Wirklichkeit* (*Form and Reality*). "*Gestalt*," writes Gilbert Merlio, "is the Form of forms, what 'informs' reality in the manner of the Aristotelian *entelechy*; it is the morphological unity that one perceives beneath the diversity of historical reality, the formative idea (or *Urpflanze!*) that gives it coherence and direction" ("Les images du guerrier chez Ernst Jünger" ["The Images of the Warrior in Ernst Jünger"], in Danièle Beltran-Vidal, ed., *Images d'Ernst Jünger* [*Images of Ernst Jünger*] [Berne: Peter Lang, 1996], p. 35).

tively neat, which makes it a kind of intermediary between the phenomenon and the figure: "It is," says Jünger, "the model image of the phenomenon and the guarantor image of the figure." The figure has a greater extension than the type. It exceeds the type, as the matrix that gives the form exceeds the form. In addition, if the type qualifies a group, the figure tends rather to qualify a reign or an epoch. Different types can coexist alongside each other in the same time and place, but there is room for only one figure. From this point of view, the relationship between the figure and the type is comparable to that of the one and the many. (This is why Jünger writes: "Monotheism can know, strictly speaking, only one figure. That is why it demotes the gods to the rank of types.") That amounts to saying that the figure is not only a more extensive type, but that there is also a difference in nature between the figure and the type. The figure can also give rise to types, assigning them a mission and a meaning. Jünger gives the example of the ocean as an expanse distinct from all the specific seas: "The ocean is formative of types; it does not have a type, it is a figure."

Can man set up a figure like he does a type? Jünger says that there is no single answer to this question, but nevertheless he tends to the negative. "The figure," he writes, "can be sustained, but not set up." This means that the figure can be neither conjured by words nor confined by thought. Whereas man can easily name types, it is much more difficult to do anything with a figure: "The risk is more significant, because one approaches the undifferentiated to a greater extent than in naming types." The type depends on man, who adapts it by naming it, whereas the figure cannot be made our own. "The naming of types," Jünger stresses, "depends on man taking possession. On the other hand, when a figure is named, we are right to suppose that it first takes possession of man." Man has no access to the "homeland of figures": "What is conceived as a figure is already configured."

Insofar as it is of the metaphysical order, a figure appears suddenly. It gives man a sign, leaving him free to ignore or *recognize* it. But man cannot grasp it by intuition alone. To know or to recognize a figure implies a more profound contact, comparable to the grasp of kinship. Jünger does not hesitate here to speak about "divination." A figure is unveiled—released from oblivion, in the Heideggerian sense; released from the deepest levels of the undifferentiated, says Jünger—by the presence of Being. But at the same time, as it reveals itself, as it rises to appearance and effective power, it "loses its essence"—like a god who chooses to incarnate himself in human form. Only this "devaluation" of its ontological status makes it possible for man to know what connects him to a figure that he cannot grasp by thought or by name. Thus the figure is the "highest representation that man can make of the ineffable and its power."

In light of the preceeding, can one say that the four Jüngerian figures are really figures and not types? Strictly speaking, only the Worker fully answers to the definition of a figure, insofar as he describes an epoch. The Soldier, the Rebel, and the Anarch would instead be types.

Jünger writes that, for man, the ability to set up types proceeds from a "magic power." He also notes that nowadays this human aptitude is declining and suggests that we are seeing the rise of the undifferentiated, i.e., a "deterioration of types," the most visible sign that the old world is giving way to a new one, whose types have not yet appeared and thus still cannot be named. "To manage to conceive new types," he writes, "the spirit must melt the old ones. . . . It is only in the glimmer of the dawn that the undifferentiated can receive new names." This is why, in the end, he wants to be optimistic: "It is foreseeable that man will recover his aptitude to set up types and will thus return to his supreme competence."

JÜNGER, HEIDEGGER, & NIHILISM*

Ernst Jünger and Martin Heidegger engaged in a dialogue on nihilism in two texts published five years apart in the 1950s on the occasion of their sixtieth birthdays.[1] The

---

* "Jünger, Heidegger et le nihilism," was originally published in *Nouvelle Ecole*, 55, 2005, pp. 121–25.

[1] Ernst Jünger, "Über die Linie" ("Across the Line"), in *Anteile: Martin Heidegger zum 60. Geburtstag* (*Parts: To Martin Heidegger on His 60th Birthday*) (Frankfurt am Main: Vittorio Klostermann, 1950), pp. 245–83; Martin Heidegger, "Über 'die Linie'" ("Regarding 'The Line'"), in Armin Mohler, ed., *Freundschaftliche Begegnungen: Festschrift für Ernst Jünger zum 60. Geburtstag* (*Friendly Encounters: Festschrift for Ernst Jünger on His 60th Birthday*) (Frankfurt am Main: Vittorio Klostermann, 1955), pp. 9–45. Jünger's text was republished separately, by the same publisher, in a slightly enlarged version: *Über die Linie* (Frankfurt am Main: Vittorio Klostermann, 1950). The French edition is *Sur l'homme et le temps, Essais* (*On Man and Time, Essays*), vol. 3, *Le nœud gordien. Passage de la ligne* (*The Gordian Knot. Crossing the Line*), trans. Henri Plard (Monaco: Rocher, 1958); 2nd expanded ed., with a Foreword by Jünger and a Preface by Julien Hervier: *Passage de la ligne* (Nantes: Passeur-Cecofop, 1993); 3rd ed. (Paris: Christian Bourgois, 1997). In English: "Across the Line," Martin Heidegger and Ernst Jünger, *Correspondence: 1949–1975*, trans. Timothy Sean Quinn (New York: Rowman and Littlefield, 2016).

Heidegger's text has also been republished separately, without modification, but under a new title: *Zur Seinsfrage* (*On the Question of Being*) (Frankfurt am Main: Vittorio Klostermann, 1956). The French edition is: "Contribution à la question de l'Etre" ("Contribution to the Question of Being"), in Martin Heidegger, *Questions* I, trans. Gérard Granel (Paris: Gallimard, 1968), pp. 195–252. The English editions are: *The Question of*

study and comparison of these texts is particularly interesting because they allow us to appreciate what, on this fundamental subject, separates two authors who are frequently compared to each other and who maintained a powerful intellectual relationship for several decades. What follows is a brief overview.

In Jünger's approach, which he carefully presents as "medical" (including "diagnosis" and "therapeutics"), he initially asserts that in order to remedy nihilism, one must give a "good definition" of it. Taking up Nietzsche's opinion that nihilism is the process in and by which "the highest values debase themselves" (*The Will to Power*), he affirms that this is essentially characterized by the devaluation then disappearance of traditional values, Christian values first and foremost.

Then Jünger reacts against the idea that nihilism is primarily a chaotic phenomenon:

> One realized, with the help of time, that nihilism can agree with vast systems of order, and that it is even generally the case, when it takes on its active form and deploys its power. It finds in order a favorable substrate; it reorganizes it towards its ends. . . . Order not only yields to the requirements of nihilism but is a component of its style. (pp. 48–52)

Being, trans. William Kluback and Jean T. Wilde (New York: Twayne, 1958) and "On the Question of Being," trans. William McNeill, in Martin Heidegger, *Pathmarks*, ed. William McNeill (Cambridge: Cambridge University Press, 1998), pp. 291–322. In Italy, the two texts were joined together in the same volume: Ernst Jünger and Martin Heidegger, *Oltre la linea*, trans. Franco Volpi and Alvise La Rocca (Milan: Adelphi, 1989). The page numbers quoted here are those of the later French editions. [We have translated Benoist's Granel translation and cited the equivalent passages in McNeill.]

In this sense, nihilism is not decadence. It does not go hand in hand with slackening, but "rather produced men who march straight ahead like iron machines, insensitive even at the moment catastrophe shatters them" (p. 57). Likewise, nihilism is not a disease. There is nothing morbid about it. On the contrary, one finds it "linked to physical health—above all, where one sets vigorously to work" (p. 54). On the other hand, nihilism is essentially reductive: its constant tendency is to "reduce the world, with its multiple and complex antagonisms, to a common denominator" (p. 65). Transforming society from "a moral community to a mechanical conglomeration" (p. 63), it marries fanaticism, the complete absence of moral sentiment, and the "perfection" of technical organization.

These observations are characteristic of Jünger. They show that whenever he mentions nihilism he refers first of all to the model of the totalitarian state, and most particularly to National Socialism. Indeed, the Third Reich exemplifies the social state where men are subject to an absolute order and "automatic" organization, in which the devaluation of all traditional morals went along with an undeniable exaltation of "health."

But one might ask if what Jünger describes really is nihilism. Is he not, rather, simply describing totalitarianism—the totalitarian Leviathan that has put technology at its bidding and turned nature into an industrial wasteland?

In addition, Jünger professes a certain optimism already apparent in the title of his text: "Across the Line." He notes that Nietzsche's and Dostoevsky's critiques of nihilism did not prevent them from being relatively optimistic, given that nihilism can be surpassed in "some time to come" (Nietzsche), and that it constitutes a kind of "necessary phase in a movement toward precise ends" (Dostoevsky). Here Jünger takes up an idea already familiar to him: after the worst, things can only get better. Or

more precisely: a tendency pushed to its extreme must
rebound in the opposite direction. Thus he said, in the
1930s, that they had "to lose the war to gain the nation." It
is in this spirit that he quotes Bernanos: "The light bursts
forth only if darkness has overrun everything. The absolute superiority of the enemy is precisely what turns
against him" (pp. 37–38). Jünger's feeling is that the worst
has passed, that "the head has crossed the line," i.e., man
has started to leave nihilism behind. This assertion also
results from his assimilation of nihilism to totalitarianism.
As Julien Hervier writes, "If Jünger believes in going beyond the absolute zero, then the collapse of Hitlerism, the
triumphant incarnation of moral nihilism, was not for
nothing" (Preface, p. 13).[2]

In his essay, Jünger thus tries primarily to describe the
state of the world as it is, in order to assess the possibility
that one has already passed to the other side of the "line."
His conclusion, moreover, might appear modest. Against
nihilism, he has recourse to the poets and to love ("Eros").
He calls for individual dissent, for "authentic anarchy." (In
1950, he had not yet arrived at the figure of the Anarch.)
"Above all," he writes, "it is necessary to find safety in

---

[2] Later on, Jünger reconsidered this optimism somewhat:
"After the defeat, I said in substance: the head of the snake already crossed the line of nihilism, and left it behind, and the
whole body soon will follow, and we will soon enter a better
spiritual climate, etc. In fact, we are far from it" (interview with
Frédéric de Towarnicki, in *Martin Heidegger* [Paris: L'Herne,
1983], p. 149). More fundamentally, Jünger thinks that we are in
a time of transition—an interregnum—and that this is why one
should not despair: "For my part, I have a presentiment that the
twenty-first century will be better than the twentieth" (*Entretiens avec Julien Hervier* [*Interviews with Julien Hervier*] [Paris:
Gallimard, 1986], p. 156). English edition: Julien Hevier, *The Details of Time: Conversation with Jünger*, trans. Joachim
Neugroschel (New York: Marsilio, 1995).

one's own heart. Then, the world will change."

Heidegger's approach is quite different. His text, written in answer to Jünger's, is above all a critique—a friendly one, of course, which stresses the regard he has for his interlocutor, but nonetheless aims at replacing his analysis with a completely different point of view.

The modification of the title is already revealing. Whereas Jünger's title "Über die Linie" means "Over the Line" in the sense of "beyond the line," Heidegger's title "Über 'die Linie'" means "regarding 'the line,'" indicating his conviction that the line has not been crossed, as well as his desire to raise the question of why it cannot yet be crossed. Thus, to Jünger's *trans lineam* topography, Heidegger explicitly states that he wants to add (and in many respects oppose) a topology *de linea*: "You examine and you go beyond the line; I am satisfied initially to consider this line you have represented. One helps the other, and vice-versa" (Granel, p. 203; McNeill, p. 294).

Heidegger starts by disputing that one can give a "good definition" of nihilism, as Jünger claims. Heidegger writes:

> While keeping to the image of the line, we discover that it traverses a space that is itself given by a site. The site gathers. The gathering shelters the gathered in its essence. It is the site of the line that gives the source of the essence of nihilism and its realization. (Granel, p. 200; McNeill, p. 292)

Thus, to inquire about the realization of nihilism, for which the entire world has become the theater—such that nihilism is henceforth the "normal state" of humanity—requires that we locate this "site of the line," which points towards the essence of nihilism. For Heidegger, to pose the question of the situation of man in relation to the movement of nihilism requires a "determination of essence." To understand nihilism implies that thought must go back to a consideration of its essence.

The answer was quick in coming. It follows from Heidegger's philosophy, the essential tenets of which I will assume here. Nihilism, in Heidegger's eyes, represents the consequence and the accomplishment of a slow trend toward the oblivion of Being, which begins with Socrates and Plato, continues in Christianity and Western metaphysics, and triumphs in modern times. The essence of nihilism "rests in the oblivion of Being" (Granel, p. 247; McNeill, p. 318). Nihilism is the oblivion of Being in realized form. It is the reign of nothingness.

The oblivion of Being means that Being is veiled, that it is held in a veiled withdrawal that conceals it from the thought of man, but which is also a protective retreat, a postponement of disclosure: "Such veiling is the essence of oblivion." Oblivion is the concealment of Being to the profit of beings. In Western metaphysics, God himself is nothing but the supreme being. Metaphysics knows only transcendence, i.e., the thought of Being. This is why it is prohibited not only to rise to Being, but even to examine its proper essence.

Heidegger adds that it is in the "reign of the will to will" that the essence of nihilism is realized. Here, of course, the target is Nietzsche. For Heidegger, the philosophy of the author of *Zarathustra* is, in spite of its merits, only Platonism in reverse, given that it does not manage to leave the realm of values. The Will to Power, analyzed by Heidegger as "will to will" (i.e., a will that wants to be in an unconditioned manner), is only one mode of appearance of the Being of beings, and in this sense another form of the oblivion of Being. "It belongs to the essence of the Will to Power," writes Heidegger, "not to allow the reality on which it establishes its power to appear in *this* reality that it itself essentially is" (Granel, p. 205; McNeill, p. 295). Nietzsche states in vain that "God is dead"; he remains in the shadow of this God whose death he proclaims.

However, insofar as Jünger himself remains within the horizon of Nietzsche's thought, Heidegger's critique of Nietzsche is also aimed at him.

Here Heidegger goes back to Jünger's famous book *The Worker*, published in 1932.[3] He emphasizes that the figure (or form, *Gestalt*) of the worker corresponds quite precisely to the figure of Zarathustra within the metaphysics of the Will to Power. His advent manifests power as a will to enthrall the world, as a "total mobilization." In *The Worker*, Jünger observes: "Technology is the means by which the figure of the worker mobilizes the world." Work is deployed on a planetary scale under the direction of the Will to Power.

Of course, Heidegger is not unaware that Jünger's view of technology had evolved. Jünger first had a revelation of the importance of technology through concrete experience: the technological battles of the First World War. He then explored, not without reason, the idea that the reign of technology would inaugurate a new age of humanity. He assimilated this reign to the domination of the figure of the Worker, thinking that only such a figure could be opposed on a worldwide scale to that of the bourgeois. On this point, Jünger was mistaken, and he later recognized his error. Lastly, his opinion of technology itself changed—perhaps under the influence of his brother, Friedrich Georg, author of *Die Perfektion der Technik* (*The Perfection of Technology*, 1946).[4] After 1945, Jünger clearly related nihilism to the "titanism" of a technology that—as a

---

[3] Ernst Jünger, *Der Arbeiter: Herrschaft und Gestalt* (*The Worker: Dominion and Form*) (Hamburg: Hanseatische Verlagsanstalt, 1932)—Ed.

[4] In English: Friedrich Georg Jünger, *The Failure of Technology: Perfection without Purpose*, trans. F. D. Wieck (Hinsdale, Ill.: Regnery, 1949)—Ed.

will to dominate the world, man, and nature—follows its own course without anything being able to stop it.[5] Technology obeys only its own rules, its most intimate law consisting in the equivalence of the possible and the desirable: all that is technologically feasible will be realized in deed.

Heidegger praises without reserve the way Jünger, first in *Total Mobilization* (1931),[6] then in *The Worker*, described what he found "in the light of the Nietzschean project of Being as Will to Power." Heidegger gives him credit for having finally realized that the reign of technical work belongs to an "active nihilism" that is henceforth deployed on a planetary scale. At the same time, however, Heidegger reproaches Jünger for not having grasped how the "Nietzschean project" continues to prohibit thought about Being, and stresses that *The Worker* "remains a work whose metaphysics is the fatherland" (Granel, p. 212; McNeill, p. 299).

Heidegger reproaches Jünger for remaining, throughout his development, in the world of the *figure* and of *values*. The figure, defined by Jünger as the "calm being" that

---

[5] In fact, even with respect to this "titanic" character of technology, Jünger remains ambiguous. On the one hand, he readily opposes the titans to the gods, and he worries about the progress of titanism (the "surge of energy"). But he also writes: "One would tend to fear that the titans can bring only misfortune, but Hölderlin himself is not of this opinion. Prometheus is the messenger of the gods and the friend of men; in Hesiod, the age of the titans is the golden age" (Foreword, 26). According to him, the twenty-first century will see *at the same time* an unprecedented rise of technology and a new "spiritualization."

[6] Ernst Jünger, *Die totale Mobilmachung* (Berlin: Verlag der Zeitkritik, 1931); English translation: "Total Mobilization," trans. Joel Golb and Richard Wolin, in Richard Wolin, ed., *The Heidegger Controversy: A Critical Reader* (New York: Columbia University Press, 1991)—Ed.

becomes apparent by giving the world form as a signet leaves its imprint, is indeed nothing but a "metaphysical power." As Heidegger emphasizes:

> The figure rests on the essential traits of a humanity which, as a *subjectum*, is at the foundation of all being. . . . It is the presence of a human type (*typus*) that constitutes the ultimate subjectivity of which the achievement of modern metaphysics marks the appearance and who offers himself in the thought of this metaphysics. (Granel, pp. 212–13; McNeill, p. 299).

No longer taking part in nihilism does not yet mean holding oneself apart from nihilism. The manner in which Jünger proposes "to exit" nihilism—"to listen to the earth," to try to know "what the earth wants," while at the same time denouncing the telluric and titanic character of technology—is in this respect revealing.

Jünger writes: "The moment when the line will be crossed will reveal to us a new turning of Being; then what really is will start to shine." Heidegger answers: "To speak about a 'turning of Being' remains a makeshift solution, and thoroughly problematic, because Being resides within the turning, so that this can never first come to 'Being' from outside" (Granel, p. 229; McNeill, p. 308).

Heidegger by no means believes that the "zero line" is from now on behind us. In his eyes, the "consummation" of nihilism does not absolutely represent the end of it:

> With the consummation of nihilism *begins* only the final stage of nihilism, whose zone will be probably of an unaccustomed breadth because it will have been dominated completely by a "normal state" and by the consolidation of this state. This is why the zero line, where the consummation reaches its end,

is not yet at all visible at the end. (Granel, pp. 209–10; McNeill, p. 297)

But he also adds that it is still an error to reason, as Jünger did, as if the "zero line" were a point external to man that man could "cross." Man *himself* is the source of the oblivion of Being. He *himself* is the "zone of the line." Heidegger adds: "In no case does the line, thought as the sign of the zone of consummated nihilism, lie in front of man as something that one can cross. Then, however, the possibilities of a *trans lineam* and such a crossing collapse" (Granel, p. 233; McNeill, p. 309).

But then, if any attempt "to cross the line" remains "condemned to a representation that itself supports the hegemony of the oblivion of Being" (Granel, p. 247; McNeill, p. 319), how can man hope to finish with nihilism? Heidegger answers: "Instead of wanting to go beyond nihilism, we must finally try to enter in meditation on its essence. This is the first step that will enable us to leave nihilism behind" (Granel, p. 247; McNeill, p. 319).

Heidegger shares Jünger's opinion that nihilism is not comparable to evil or a disease. But he gives significance to this observation. When he asserts that "the essence of nihilism is not nihilistic" (Granel, p. 207; McNeill, p. 296), he means that the zone of the most extreme danger is also that which saves. The disease can also point towards the cure.

"To enter in meditation" on the essence of nihilism means giving oneself the possibility of an appropriation (*Verwindung*) of metaphysics. The appropriation of metaphysics is indeed also appropriation of the oblivion of Being—and consequently the possibility of a non-concealment, of a revealing of the truth (*aletheia*). Jünger wrote that "the difficulty in defining nihilism means that the spirit is unable to represent nothing" (p. 47). Heidegger quotes this sentence to stress the proximity of

Being and the essence of nothingness. From this he argues that it is by a meditation on nothing that we will understand what nihilism is, and that it is when we understand what nihilism is that we will be able to overcome the oblivion of Being. Heidegger writes:

Nothing, even if we understand it only in the sense of the total lack of being, belongs, as absence, to presence as one of its possibilities. Consequently it is nothingness that reigns in the essence of nihilism and the essence of nothingness belongs to Being. If in addition Being is the destiny of transcendence, it is then the essence of metaphysics that is shown as the place of the essence of nihilism. (Granel, p. 236; McNeill, pp. 312–13)

The place of the essence of consummate nihilism is thus to be sought "where the essence of metaphysics deploys its extreme possibilities and gathers itself in them" (Granel, p. 236; McNeill, p. 313). Finally, Heidegger writes, "going beyond nihilism requires that one enter its essence, which, when entered, nullifies the will to go beyond. The appropriation of metaphysics calls thought to a more fundamental recall" (Granel, p. 250; McNeill, p. 320).

However, to jump the "barrier" that prevents us from entering meditatively into the essence of nihilism, it is still necessary to have a word likely to give access to the thought of Being. It is necessary, in other words, to give up the language of metaphysics—which is still that of the Will to Power, value, and the figure—because it is precisely this language that prohibits access. Heidegger is emphatic:

The only way in which we can reflect upon the essence of nihilism is initially to take the path that leads to the location of the residence of Being. It is only on this path that the question of nothingness can be located. But the question of the residence of Being withers if it does not abandon the language of metaphysics, because the metaphysical representation prohibits thinking the question of the residence of Being. (Granel, p. 225; McNeill, p. 306)

However, it is precisely there that Heidegger reproaches Jünger: he reproaches him for asking about nihilism in terms of thought and discourse that remain tributaries to the essence of metaphysics. Insofar as he continues to think and express himself in the language of metaphysics, which is the place of the essence of nihilism, Jünger makes it impossible to solve the problem he himself has posed. Heidegger asks:

In which language speaks the thought whose fundamental plan sketches a crossing of the line? Must the language of the metaphysics of the Will to Power, of the figure, and of value be still preserved on the other side of the critical line? And is the language of metaphysics, and this metaphysics itself (whether it is of the living God or the dead God) constituted *as* metaphysics, precisely the barrier that prohibits the passage of the line, i.e., the passage beyond nihilism? (Granel, pp. 224–25; McNeill, p. 306)

Thus, we cannot enter the essence of nihilism as long as we continue to express ourselves in its language. This is why Heidegger calls for a "change of saying," for a "change in the relation to the essence of speech." He calls for a saying that is necessary to overcome the oblivion of Being. Because this saying corresponds to the essence of Being, it can make Being's essence accessible to thought. It invites Being "to say thought," while specifying that "this saying is not the expression of thought, but is thought itself, its course and its song" (Granel, p. 249; McNeill, p. 320). It is necessary, he concludes, to make a "test of saying which is that of faithful thought." It is necessary "to work on the path."

How to conclude? I spoke of a "dialogue" between Jünger and Heidegger in connection with nihilism, but this term is not completely appropriate. Heidegger and Jünger often depart from analogous premises, but they arrive at somewhat opposing conclusions. They both agree that nihilism finds its most solid support in modern technology, but they do not have the same conception of it. For Jünger, technology is above all "titanic" in essence, whereas for Heidegger it is realized metaphysics. Jünger sees in nihilism the opposite of the values of Western and Christian metaphysics. Heidegger sees it as the ultimate consequence of these same values. Jünger is limited to knowing if man, in his relationship with nihilism, has "crossed the line." Heidegger invites us to wonder about what "crossing" means. In fact, Heidegger presses Jünger's work to go further and deeper, to enlarge the perspective of reflection, to invite thought to its own distinct transformation. Jünger suggested a "recourse to the forests" for the "Rebels." Heidegger invites us to take a forest path that leads to the *clearing* (*Lichtung*) where the truth (*aletheia*, unconcealment), finally leaves oblivion—i.e., this millennial erring that has governed the history of Europe, the planetary consummation of which enjoins us today to think of a way out.

THE JÜNGER–HEIDEGGER
CORRESPONDENCE*

When two great men—the greatest philosopher of the twentieth century and one of its most important writers—correspond with one another, what do they discuss? Not always great things: they also exchange pleasantries and speak of their publications, travels, and trivial preoccupations. But sometimes the tone rises. And sometimes it becomes sublime, as in 1956 when Jünger consulted Heidegger about the exact meaning of a maxim of Rivarol and received a veritable course in philosophy, stupefying in depth, on the concepts of time and movement.

Ernst Jünger and Martin Heidegger began corresponding in 1949 regarding plans for a journal called *Pallas*, to be edited by the essayist Armin Mohler (who was Jünger's private secretary from 1949 to 1953). This project came to nothing—but subsequently Jünger, along with the historian of religions Mircea Eliade, created another journal called *Antaios*. Their correspondence continued until Heidegger's death in May 1976. Published in Germany in 2008, it is now available in French, beautifully translated, edited, and annotated by Julien Hervier.[1] It

---

* Originally published as "Jünger et Heidegger. Deux géants dans le siècle," in *Le Choc du mois*, May 2010, pp. 46–47.

[1] Ernst Jünger and Martin Heidegger, *Correspondance 1949–1975*, ed. and trans. Julien Hervier (Paris: Christian Bourgois, 2010). In English: Martin Heidegger and Ernst Jünger, *Correspondence: 1949–1975*, trans. Timothy Sean Quinn (New York: Rowman and Littlefield, 2016).

It is worth nothing that a good dozen volumes gathering the letters exchanged by Jünger with his principal correspondents have appeared in Germany in recent years. I would like to see translations of some of these, in particular his correspond-

offers a rare kind of pleasure.

Jünger first met Heidegger at the end of 1948 in his hut in the forest at Todtnauberg. Later Jünger wrote: "From the beginning, there was something—not only something beyond word and thought, but beyond the man himself" (*Rivarol and Other Essays*). This was the immediate postwar period, a sad and painful time when the two men were treated as if they were radioactive. Jünger, on June 25th, 1949, wrote this superb sentence: "In the course of these last years, it has become quite clear to me that silence is the strongest of weapons, provided that it is dissimulated behind something that deserves to be hushed up."

But what is most striking about these letters is the difference in tone between the philosopher and the writer. Both men genuinely admired one another, but intellectually Heidegger completely dominated his interlocutor. Jünger does not offer the slightest criticism of Heidegger, but the reverse is not entirely the case.

Indeed, Jünger—unlike his brother Friedrich Georg Jünger—did not have a genuinely philosophical mind. He lets on that Heidegger's works, about which he knew little, were sometimes above his head. In November 1967, he noted: "Your texts are difficult and hardly translatable: thus, I am always astonished by the influence they exert on the intelligent French." Everything indicates that Jünger had been more impressed by Heidegger's intellectual charisma than by his thought. He was also more inclined to pay visits, more eager to maintain relations with his contemporary. Heidegger was more reluctant to move, more estranged from "social" life—more concerned about the essential. As Lao-Tzu said about the sage: "He does not act, but he accomplishes."

---

ence with Friedrich Hielscher (2005) and above all Carl Schmitt (2006). This last volume runs to nearly one thousand pages.

Heidegger, moreover, said explicitly that in his eyes Jünger was not "thinker" (*Denker*). He was a man who theorized based on his experience, on what he saw and lived (beginning with his experiences in the trenches of the First World War), but not from what can only be thought. Jünger, in other words, had *ideas* more than he had *thought*. He was an "*Erkenner*," a man who "recognizes," more concerned to open up "new optics" than to arrive at "new truths." This is why Heidegger writes:

> He [Jünger] does not have the slightest idea of what occurs in the "objectification" of the world and man. Ultimately his knowledge remains psychological and moral. . . . He always remains within metaphysics. . . . Because Jünger does not see what is uniquely "thinkable," he regards the fulfillment of metaphysics as the essence of the Will to Power as the dawn of a new era, whereas it constitutes only a prelude to the rapid decrepitude of all recent innovations, destined to founder in the ennui of a nothingness of insignificance that incubates this abandonment of Being that is proper to beings.

Difficult language? There's more.

Heidegger, in any case, was interested in Jünger for a long time. In 1932, *The Worker*, the great theoretical book of the veteran of the front, held Heidegger's attention like few other works. During the winter semester 1939–40 at the University of Freiburg, Heidegger even devoted a whole seminar to this book. The texts that he wrote on Jünger, collected together in a volume of almost 500 pages published in Germany in 2004 (volume 90 of his complete works, still in the course of publication by Vittorio Klostermann), testify eloquently.

In Jünger, Heidegger admired someone who had understood the world based on the Will to Power and had clarified the role played by technology in this perspective. The figure of the Worker is indeed present in the world in the form of power. It is through the figure of the Worker that technology, as engine and instrument, brings about "total mobilization." In a direct reference to *The Worker* Heidegger wrote: "Work . . . today rises to the metaphysical rank of this unconditional objectification of all things present, which deploys its being in the will to will" (*Vorträge und Aufsätze*).

Heidegger was an admiring reader of Jünger, but also a critical one. The dialogue the two men maintained, often indirectly, proves this unambiguously. The best way to appreciate what separates them is to read side by side the texts they dedicated to one another on their respective 60th birthdays: Jünger's "Over the Line" (*Über die Linie*), (1950) and Heidegger's "Regarding 'The Line'" (*Über « die Linie »*) (1955). Both texts deal with the essence of modern technology and the light it throws on the concept of nihilism. It is noteworthy that Nietzsche constitutes the central axis of the dialogue between Heidegger and Jünger.

In his text of 1950, Jünger in effect takes Nietzsche's thought as the starting point for a tentative evaluation of contemporary nihilism. He concludes with a kind of optimism that the worst has passed. The modern world, he says, has passed the "zero point," i.e., the watershed of nihilism. Heidegger affirms, on the contrary, that this world is more than ever plunged into the "oblivion of Being" that cannot be escaped unless one abandons the language of metaphysics ("the zero line, where the fulfillment reaches the end, is ultimately the least visible of all").

Without going too far into abstract details, a summary is necessary here. In the two large volumes collecting his lecture courses on Nietzsche (1936–46), Heidegger claims that although the author of *Thus Spoke Zarathustra* closes the circle of Western metaphysics, he nevertheless remains locked inside it. The Will to Power, in his eyes, is only the "will to will," i.e., exacerbated subjectivity (it is a "will to itself," a will that depends on itself at the same time as it is posited as its own object). The modern epoch of decline is that of the completion of metaphysics in the form of the metaphysics of the will, of which Nietzsche is the last representative. For Nietzsche, ultimately, "power and will have the same meaning." Heidegger invites Jünger to think beyond the Nietzschean metaphysics of the Will to Power, the modern metaphysics of subjectivity upon which he continues to depend.

Heidegger has nothing but the highest opinion of Nietzsche. And of Jünger. He only invites him to think further. Ernst Jünger, it should also be emphasized, is one of the very rare authors with whom Heidegger agreed, after 1945, to maintain a continued dialogue, which is assuredly not nothing.

For the 80th birthday of the author of *Storm of Steel*, Heidegger sent this message to him: "Remain with the luminous spirit of decision that you have always demonstrated in the quite distinct way in which you speak." One imagines that this sort of remark would be badly conveyed today by text message or email!

Jünger & Drieu[*]

In his *Pariser Tagebücher* (*Paris Diaries*), Ernst Jünger refers to his meetings in German-occupied Paris with Pierre Drieu La Rochelle (e.g., on October 11th, 1941, and on April 7th, 1942).[1] Drieu was then the editor-in-chief of *La Nouvelle Revue Française*, published by Gallimard. On Thursdays, Jünger often attended the literary salon of Florence Gould, to which Gerhard Heller introduced him, and where he became acquainted with Paul Léautaud, Henry de Montherlant, Marcel Jouhandeau, Alfred Fabre-Luce, Jean Schlumberger, Jean Cocteau, Paul Morand, Jean Giraudoux, and many others. Later, Jouhandeau would remember him as a "very simple man, very young looking, with a delicate face, who wore civilian clothing and a bow tie."[2]

On November 16, 1943, Jünger noted in his journal that he had again seen Drieu La Rochelle at the German Institute of Paris, then directed by Karl Epting. He told him that they had "exchanged fire in 1915. It was near Godat, the village where Hermann Löns fell. Drieu also remembered the bell that sounded the hours there: we both heard it." Many years later, in his discussions with

[*] Originally published as "Jünger et Drieu," in *Ernst Jünger entre les dieux et les titans* (Le Chesnay: Vira Romana, 2020), pp. 131–43.

[1] Ernst Jünger, *A German Officer in Occupied Paris: The War Journals, 1941–1945*, trans. Thomas S. Hansen and Abby J. Hansen (New York: Columbia University Press, 2019), pp. 23–23, 62—Ed.

[2] Marcel Jouhandeau, "Mon ami Ernst Jünger" ("My friend Ernst Jünger"), in *Hommage à Ernst Jünger* (*Homage to Ernst Jünger*), ed. Georges Laffly, special issue of *La Table ronde*, Winter 1976, p. 9.

Antonio Gnoli and Franco Volpi, Jünger, now 100 years old, recalled this event again: "When we met, we often spoke about our experiences of the First World War: we had fought in the same zone of the front, he on the French side, I on the German side, and we heard, on opposite sides, the sound of the bells of the same church."[3]

It should be no surprise that the two men were drawn together initially by their memories of the Great War. It had marked them deeper than anything else, like so many men of their generation. But between Jünger and Drieu La Rochelle, there were many other points in common. Deeply impressed by the reading of Nietzsche, both aspired to an African adventure in their youth: Jünger enlisted in the French Foreign Legion, while in 1914 Drieu requested to be assigned to the Moroccan riflemen (in both cases, the experience was brief). Above all, both men were political theorists as well as writers—simultaneously in the case of Drieu, successively in that of Jünger. Both justifiably could be described at one point in their lives or another as "national revolutionaries." Finally, both were incontestably revolutionary conservatives, eager to safeguard values that they considered eternal, at the same time conscious that the advent of the modern world created chasms across which one cannot turn back. Yet, despite all that, many things separated them.

Jünger described the First World War almost while under fire, whereas Drieu waited twenty years to write *La comédie de Charleroi*.[4] (Moreover, having been discharged in 1939, Drieu did not take part in the Second

---

[3] Ernst Jünger, *Les prochains Titans* (*The Coming Titans*) (Paris: Grasset, 1998), p. 99.

[4] Pierre Drieu La Rochelle, *The Comedy of Charleroi and Other Stories*, trans. Douglas Gallagher (Cambridge: Rivers Press, 1973)—Ed.

World War.) In the first of the six short stories of *La comédie de Charleroi*, which is certainly one of Drieu's mas-
terpieces, he recalls an assault against the Germans in
1914 in the area of Charleroi. This description is made
within the framework of a visit to the battlefield made
five years later by the narrator in the company of a rich
bourgeois who lost his son in this battle. One notes that
twenty years later, beyond any ideological justification,
Jünger and Drieu perceived war as a law inherent in human nature, even as a rehabilitation of "natural man" in
the totality of his instincts. "It is life in the most terrible
form that the creator ever gave it," Jünger wrote.[5] For
Drieu as for Jünger, war is first of all what frees us from
the bourgeois world and reveals man in his truth.

However, both also noted how much the Great War,
which began in 1914 as a traditional war, had been transformed little by little into a war of a completely new type:
a deployment of gigantically impersonal forces, a "duel of
machines so formidable that beside them man no longer
exists, so to speak."[6] But the advent of "technical war"
particularly horrified Drieu, who saw it as a "malevolent
revolt of matter against human control," a true "industrial butchery," whereas for Jünger it gave birth to the intuition of a new human type, completely opposed to the
bourgeois: the Worker, whose "heroic realism" would be
able to ensure the mobilization (*Mobilmachung*) of the
world. For Jünger, the "armies of machines" herald the
"battalions of workmen," the experience of the war having conferred on man a disposition (*Bereitschaft*) to "total mobilization," i.e., a will to domination (*Herrschaft*)
expressed by means of technology.

Drieu shares nothing of this optimistic and volunta-

---

[5] Ernst Jünger, *Le combat comme expérience intérieure*, trans.
François Poncet (Paris: Christian Bourgois, 1997), p. 244.

[6] *Le combat comme experience intérieure*, p. 243.

rist vision. In the inter-war period, he opposed an ethics that continued to preach the old "warlike values" without realizing that these values have no worse enemy than modern war. "Modern war is in every way an abomination," he wrote in 1934 in *Socialisme fasciste* (*Fascist Socialism*).[7] According to Drieu, the reign of technology, far from heralding the advent of a new man, implies on the contrary a degradation of man. As is well-known, it was only later, under the double influence of Heidegger and Friedrich Georg Jünger, that Ernst Jünger began to reflect critically on technology and its "titanic" nature, extending and deepening the purely instinctive reaction of Drieu.

After having served on the front, which brought a kind of mystical experience, both writers believed it possible to retain what they had acquired on the battlefield in civilian life. "We will be able to establish peace like we carried out the war," Drieu wrote in its first book, a collection of poems entitled *Interrogation*.[8] At the same time, Jünger also resolved to transform military defeat into civilian victory. This resolution explains his political commitment.

Their relationship to politics, however, is not the same. In the 1920s, Jünger joined the ranks of the nationalists out of deep and fiery convictions. Drieu, however, plunged in to ward off his own hesitatancy. The author of *Le Feu follet* (*The Will o' the Wisp*)[9] belongs to those men who came to politics starting from philosophy, with the need to find concrete incarnations of ideas corre-

---

[7] Pierre Drieu La Rochelle, *Socialisme fasciste* (Paris: Gallimard, 1934)—Ed.

[8] Pierre Drieu La Rochelle, *Interrogation* (Paris: Gallimard, 1917)—Ed.

[9] Pierre Drieu La Rochelle, *Le Feu Follet* (Paris: Gallimard, 1931). English translation, *The Will o' the Wisp*, trans. Robinson Martin (London: Calder and Boyars, 1966)—Ed.

sponding to their vision of the world. More than an actor, Drieu wanted to be an observer. During the Great War, moreover, whereas Jünger was completely engaged in the "storm of steel," Drieu was in combat only intermittently, although that did not prevent him from being wounded three times.

In many respects, Drieu was a dilettante. Regarding his *Journal* of the years 1939–1945, which was published only in 1992, one can even speak about his "indifference to any deep ideological conviction," of his "fickleness" (Julien Hervier). This is not inaccurate, but one absolutely should not see the least trace of opportunism in this attitude. Germanophile but Anglomaniac, haunted by decadence but conscious that his own work fits a certain definition of it, Drieu is a man of doubts, about-face changes, and oscillations—perhaps manifesting his bourgeois origins.

One sees this clearly in his relations with women. The author of a beautiful novel entitled *L'homme couvert de femmes* (*The Man Covered with Women*, 1925),[10] which may be largely autobiographical, Drieu loved women, but not for themselves. His Don Juanism, of quasi-Platonic inspiration, is articulated around the desire to seduce, as well as the "insane idea of beauty": "Impossible for me to attach to a woman, impossible for me to abandon her. I found none of them beautiful enough. Beautiful enough internally or externally."[11] This is why this man "covered with women" was always lonely. The same applied to politics: no political regime could attract him completely, just as no woman was sufficiently "beautiful" for him.

But it is precisely because he is attracted by an unat-

---

[10] Pierre Drieu La Rochelle, *L'homme couvert de femmes* (Paris: Gallimard, 1935)—Ed.

[11] Pierre Drieu La Rochelle, *Journal* (Paris: Gallimard, 1992), p. 512.

tainable ideal and perpetually divided between contradictory impulses that Pierre Drieu La Rochelle did not
cease fighting against what he regarded as false alternatives. *Interrogation* contains the poem "And Dreams and
Action." The juxtaposition of these two words translates
quite precisely what he sought to reconcile all his life.
Drieu wanted to reconcile dream and action, as he wanted to reconcile soul and body, the world of war and that
of the spirit.

He interpreted the history of Europe as the slow rise
of the bourgeois ideology which led to the rupture of
equilibrium between soul and body and subjected man
to the noxious influence of life in the big cities. His great
task was the reconciliation of the soul and the body. In
his *Notes pour comprendre le siècle* (*Notes to Comprehend the Century*, 1941),[12] he writes: "The new man participates in the body, he knows that the body is the articu-
lation of the soul, and that the soul cannot be expressed,
cannot deploy itself, except though the body."

Drieu's attitude is that of a dandy. Yet many authors
also saw Jünger as a rather typical representative of dandyism. Nicolas Sombart writes:

> The dandy represents the type of man who stylizes
> himself. . . . He has sublimated the Will to Power
> into a will to style. . . . Endeavoring to stylize him-
> self, he stylizes the world and accomplishes this
> mission when he captures a situation in an elegant
> formulation. . . . For that, he must subject himself
> to discipline, abnegation, and rigorous asceticism.[13]

---

[12] Pierre Drieu La Rochelle, *Notes pour comprendre le siècle*
(Paris: Gallimard, 1941)—Ed.

[13] Nicolas Sombart, "Le dandy dans sa maison forestière: re-
marques sur le cas Ernst Jünger" ("The Dandy in His Forest
House: Remarks on the Case of Ernst Jünger"), in *Ernst Jünger,*

"Distance, beauty, impassibility, such are the elements of Jüngerian dandyism," writes Julien Hervier for his part.[14] One thinks here of the ideal of "active impersonality" preached by another theorist of dandyism, the Italian Julius Evola. However, Drieu is more of a dandy than Jünger, because the former preaches "engagement for engagement's sake," as others might speak of "art for art's sake."

Drieu gives history the same impassioned attention that Jünger gives botany or entomology. But for him, history is essentially in flux, governed by chance, whereas Jünger strives to read, behind surface appearances and movement, the "harmonious permanence of a stable order" (Julien Hervier). In Jünger, history is never a purely human phenomenon. Instead, it traces back to an invisible necessity, a kind of metaphysics of destiny, of forces that exceed it. This is why Jünger is not interested so much in history as in what lies beyond history. That is why he is interested in myth.

Drieu, who had dreamed of becoming a priest or monk, and who, in the Foreword of one of his more famous novels, *Gilles* (1939),[15] wrote that if he could re-live his life, he would devote it to the history of religion, was also passionately interested in myth. Like Jünger, he refers constantly to the sacred, but never tries to relate it to a particular religion. For him, the sacred is synonymous with the divine, and the divine is more immanent that transcendent.

He was already using religious terms to describe the

---

ed. Philippe Barthelet (Lausanne: L'Age d'Homme, 2000), p. 396.

[14] Julien Hervier, *Deux individus contre l'histoire: Drieu La Rochelle, Ernst Jünger* (*Two Individuals against History: Drieu La Rochelle, Ernst Jünger*) (Paris: Klincksieck, 1978), p. 86.

[15] Pierre Drieu La Rochelle, *Gilles* (Paris: Gallimard, 1939)— Ed.

brutal reality of the Great War. When the bombs burst, he exclaimed: "These are not men, it is the Good god, the Good god himself, the Hard one, the Brutal one!" (*La comédie de Charleroi*). For him, the war was just like religion: a sacred kind of test. Everywhere in his work, the bond between the soldier's life and asceticism, the bond between action and religion, is manifest.

Finally, Drieu, like Jünger—who says that the cosmos for him has a divine and sacred dimension—holds that "nature is animated, speaking, innumerably prodigious." Jünger seldom employs the word "God," unlike Drieu, who uses it frequently. But, from Nietzsche's claim that "God is dead," he draws the conviction that "God must be conceived in a new way."

Jünger definitively moved away from politics in the early 1930s, while Drieu was never detached. As Julien Hervier notes, the need for engagement leads Drieu to an ethics of action for action's sake. Under the Occupation, it is this concern with engagement on principle that led him to continue to write political articles although politics hardly interested him anymore. Reading his journal, one sees that his true interests inclined him toward Eastern spirituality.

It amounts to saying that for Drieu, politics was never more than "a reason for curiosity and the object of distant speculation" which never exercised more than a "fitful" attraction.[16] Rejecting the bourgeois and democratic world, he certainly never creased believing in the possibility of a non-Marxist socialism. But in his fashion, i.e., "by fits and starts," and not without a certain blindness to the reality of things.

Jünger withdrew from politics because he took the full measure of the "Mauritanian" spirit, whereas Drieu, on the contrary, continued his engagement because he

---

[16] *Journal*, pp. 437 and 309.

thought that in life, one is obliged to get one's hands dirty. By adopting this attitude, the dandy saves himself relative to the collapse he observes all around him. When the battle is lost, there remains only the beauty of the gesture.

At the end of the Second World War, Drieu felt he was watching the end of a world, the end of an era: "France is finished. . . . But all the fatherlands are finished." One should, however, recall that he constantly pled for Europe. In 1931, he published a book entitled *L'Europe contre les patries (Europe against the Fatherlands).*[17] In 1934, in *La comédie de Charleroi*, he wrote: "Today, France or Germany, it is too small."

Jünger—who was always a Francophile, as Drieu was a Germanophile—also knew how to step back from narrow national memberships: *Der Arbeiter* already poses the problem of globalism that after the war Jünger discussed in his essay on the universal state.

Drieu dreamed only of regeneration. Like Nietzsche, he thinks one should not seek to save what is crumbling but instead accelerate its collapse. In his journal, he declares that he desires the destruction of the West and calls for a barbarian invasion that will sweep away this dying civilization: "It is with joy that I greet the rise of Russia and Communism. It will be atrocious, atrociously destructive."[18]

At the same time, he also wrote: "I regarded Fascism only as a step towards Communism." The ease with which Drieu praised Stalinist Communism as well as Fascism or National Socialism, placing on the former the quickly disappointed hopes inspired by the latter, will surprise only those who are entirely ignorant of National

---

[17] Pierre Drieu La Rochelle, *L'Europe contre les patries* (Paris: Gallimard, 1931)—Ed.

[18] *Journal*, p. 379.

Bolshevism, incarnated for example by Ernst Niekisch, who was a very close friend of Jünger's in the 1920s.

In his youth, under Niekisch's influence, Jünger also saw the Communists as the best preparers of the "revolution without qualifications"[19] that he would celebrate in *Der Arbeiter*. Later, but from an entirely different viewpoint, he would emphasize the extent to which Communism and National Socialism paralleled each other in the introduction of technology into political life, thus expressing a common adhesion to modernity, under the horizon of a Will to Power that Heidegger had unmasked as a mere "will to will." One finds similar reflections in *Genève ou Moscou* (*Geneva or Moscow*, 1928),[20] where Drieu stresses that capitalism and communism are the twin heirs of the Machine: "Both are the dark and burning children of industry."[21]

However, Drieu was at the same time tempted by retreat, by retiring to the sidelines. One of his last novels, *L'homme à cheval* (*The Man on Horseback*),[22] published in 1943, tells the story of a South American dictator, Jaime Torrijos, who, after having seized power in Bolivia, tried to create an empire. Unable to attain this goal, he retires from politics to resuscitate the Inca rites.

Like the hero of *L'homme à cheval*, Drieu dreamed "of something deeper than politics, or rather that deep and rare politics that fuses with poetry, music, and—who knows?—perhaps high religion." But he did not know how to proceed in that direction. Perhaps he did not have in him the resources that would have enabled him

---

[19] *Die Standarte*, November 23, 1925.

[20] Pierre Drieu La Rochelle, *Genève ou Moscou* (Paris: Gallimard, 1928)—Ed.

[21] *Genève ou Moscou*, p. 131.

[22] Pierre Drieu La Rochelle, *L'homme à cheval* (Paris: Gallimard, 1943).

to become a *Waldgänger* or Anarch.

Jünger also had the feeling that an epoch in world history was completed. It was completed with the appearance of the Worker, who inaugurated the global reign of "the elemental." The old gods died or fled; the new gods are yet to be born. We have entered the era of the titans. To step back, Jünger successively created the figure (*Gestalt*) of the *Waldgänger*, who takes a distance, then that of the Anarch, who takes height.

The attitude of the Anarch is similar in some respects to the *apoliteia* preached by Julius Evola. But this figure, like that of the *Waldgänger*, clearly poses the problem of the place of the individual in relation to the great historical processes that affect the world. Jünger evokes in this respect "the individual taken separately, the great solitary, able to resist the spiritual challenges of that which is heralded and will become a new 'Iron Age.'"[23]

One could speak here of a Jüngerian "individualism." Jünger's individualism is certainly not hedonistic individualism, which reflects the selfishness and the utilitarianism of the bourgeois world, but rather the assertion of the prerogatives of the isolated individual (*der Einzelne*) who can spontaneously recognize others of his kind.

In Drieu La Rochelle, on the other hand, there are unquestionable traces of this bourgeois individualism, which he energetically condemns from the historical point of view, but which he does not always manage to escape himself. The majority of his novels are nothing more than stories about individuals, and his characters are quite often mere expressions of himself. Also, both writers give different roles to individuals and elites. While Drieu aspires to a new political aristocracy, Jünger is situated on a higher plane: the spiritual accord that can be established between men able to spiritually dom-

---

[23] *Les prochains Titans*, p. 102.

inate their time.

Just like Henry de Montherlant, Yukio Mishima, and so many others, Pierre Drieu La Rochelle finally committed suicide. But one would be wrong to explain his suicide merely as a political defeat, even if he himself encouraged this by saying, in substance: "I played, I lost, I claim death." In fact, Drieu had been tempted by suicide since childhood. He had written: "When I was an adolescent, I promised myself to remain faithful to youth: one day, I tried to keep my word." In dying, like the hero of his novel *Le feu follet*, Drieu remained faithful to this temptation from his childhood. Previously, he had written in his journal: "The beauty of death consoles a life badly lived. God, what was my life? Some women, the charge of Charleroi, some words, viewing some landscapes, statues, tableaux, and that's it."[24]

Ernst Jünger wrote that "suicide belongs to the capital of humanity," and it is a maxim that Montherlant had noted in his notebooks when he himself decided to commit suicide in September 1972. Jünger also saw many close friends commit suicide, particularly at the time of the July 1944 assassination attempt against Hitler (Hans von Kluge, Henrich von Stülpnagel) and at the end of the Second World War. But for him suicide remained an abstract possibility, negative in its essence, while for Drieu, for whom death was "the secret of life," suicide had a mystical value.

On September 7th, 1944, when he was in Kirchhorst, Jünger learned that Drieu had committed suicide in Paris. "It seems," he wrote, "that under the terms of some law, those who had noble reasons to cultivate friendship between peoples fall without mercy, while the low profiteers wriggle away."[25] In his conversations with Julien

---

[24] *Journal*, p. 304.
[25] *A German Officer in Occupied Paris*, p. 346—Ed.

Hervier, he later said that he was "deeply distressed" that Drieu "committed suicide in a moment of despair." "His death," he added, "truly pained me. He was a man who had suffered much. Thus, there are people who feel friendship for a certain nation, as many Frenchmen came to feel for us, which brought them no luck."[26] On September 6th, 1992, he wrote to Julien Hervier: "Gallimard sent me your edition of Drieu's diaries; reading them was moving. The critics have, so far as I know, not grasped the significance of his work. I have made some notes on it for *Siebzig verweht IV*. A copy is enclosed."

Words to remember. Between these two men, there was brotherhood.

---

[26] Julien Hervier, *Entretiens avec Ernst Jünger* (Paris: Gallimard, 1986), p. 127. In English: Julien Hervier, *The Details of Time: Conversations with Ernst Jünger*, trans. Joachim Neugroschel (New York: Marsilio, 1995), p. 106.

ERNST JÜNGER & THE FRENCH NEW RIGHT*

The New Right obviously did not have to introduce Ernst Jünger in France. When the New Right appeared at the end of the 1960s, the author of *On the Marble Cliffs* was already well-known to the French public. Indeed, Jünger was surely the German writer most famous and most read on this side of the Rhine. This situation, which always astonishes the Germans, has multiple explanations.

First of all, Jünger was translated relatively early: his principal works on the First World War appeared at the beginning of the 1930s, and they immediately made him famous.[1] But above all, France played a leading role in Jünger's career, as well as in his life and in his spiritual and literary formation. Since his youthful escapade in the Foreign Legion, since the terrible experience of the trenches, France never ceased to occupy a significant place in Jünger's heart, evident in the many relations he maintained with French people, his reading of Barrès or Leon Bloy, but also the translations that he himself made of the *Maxims* of Rivarol or texts by Guy de Maupassant and Paul Léautaud.

Finally, Jünger had the good fortune to always find

---

* Originally published as "Ernst Jünger et la Nouvelle Droite française," in *Ernst Jünger entre les dieux et les titans* (Le Chesnay: Vira Romana, 2020), pp. 144–55.

[1] *Orages d'acier. Souvenirs du front de France* (*In Stahlgewittern* [*Storm of Steel*]) (Paris: Payot, 1930); *Le boqueteau 125. Chronique des combats des tranchées 1918* (*Das Wäldchen 125* [*Copse 125*]) (Paris: Payot, 1932); *La guerre notre mère* (*Der Kampf als inneres Erlebnis* [*Battle as Inner Experience*]) (Paris: Albin Michel, 1934).

French translators of great talent, from Henri Thomas and Henri Plard to Julien Hervier and François Poncet, who were acutely sensitive to his style and to his thought and were thus able to render all their nuances.

"I think," said Jünger in 1973, "that the French can appreciate when a German presents himself as he is, instead of seeking at all costs to assume a face that is not his own."[2]

This celebrity, however, was won over a long time only at the price of a certain ambiguity. At least until around 1975, the French perceived Ernst Jünger as a figure belonging exclusively to the literary world. Of course, the politico-historical background of his work was known, but he did not seem to be an actor in this period. Regarding his sojourn in Paris under the Occupation, for the most part only his literary acquaintances were remembered (Jean Cocteau, Paul Morand, Pierre Drieu La Rochelle, Sacha Guitry, Jean Giraudoux, Henry de Montherlant, Jean Schlumberger, etc.), most of whom were connected to the salon of Florence Gould. Hadn't Jünger himself described Paris as "the great city of books"?[3] His youthful political writings were completely ignored, at least by the general public. The names of Franz Schauwecker, Hugo Fischer, Ernst Niekisch, Friedrich Hielscher, and even Carl Schmitt were also unknown. In short, Jünger was seen as a writer and nothing else. Moreover, Jünger himself was apparently not only quite satisfied with this situation but contributed to it in his own way, since he long refused to allow a French translation of his great book of 1932, *Der Arbeiter*.

---

[2] "Jünger s'explique" ("Jünger Explained"), interview with Jean-Louis de Rambures, *Le Monde*, February 22, 1973.

[3] Ernst Jünger, *Journal parisien* (*Pariser Tagebuch*), July 16, 1942. In English: Ernst Jünger, *A German Officer in Occupied Paris: The War Journals, 1941–1945*, trans. Thomas S. Hansen and Abby J. Hansen (New York: Columbia University Press, 2019), p. 76.

However, it was precisely his untranslated books—
which as a consequence had a kind of mythical aura—that
quickly attracted the interest of the New Right. From the
beginning of the 1960s, I myself knew only Jünger's books
that had already been published in French. I had read, of
course, his accounts of the First World War, but—perhaps
unlike some of my friends—they had not impressed me,
surely because of my lack of interest in military matters.
On the Marble Cliffs (*Auf den Marmorklippen*) and *African
Games* (*Afrikanische Spiele*) had interested me more, as
did *Heliopolis* and especially the *Treatise of the Rebel* or
the *Recourse to the Forests* (*Der Waldgang*). *The Universal
State* (*Der Weltstaat*), on the other hand, rather repelled
me.

Obviously, I owe the discovery of the "other Jünger" to
my friend Armin Mohler. His *Handbuch der Konservative
Revolution,* that I tried to decipher with my then rudimen-
tary German, was a revelation. In this vast movement with
its innumerable ramifications, I by no means saw a current of thought that was merely a *Wegbereiter* with National Socialism, as has sometimes been said, but on the
contrary, an alternative course whose development could
perhaps have saved the world from the disaster of Hitler.

In our conversations, Armin Mohler often spoke about
Jünger, for whom he had served as private secretary for
several years after the war, and about whom, based on this
experience, he nourished rather ambivalent feelings.
Whereas I found the young conservative movement the
most interesting, politically and intellectually, Mohler did
not hide his predilection for the national revolutionary
current. I was more reserved than he on the intrinsic value
of the concepts of "nation" and "movement," but the idea
of revolution undeniably seduced me.

Thanks to Mohler, I discovered that Jünger had collaborated in "neo-nationalist" or *bündisch* journals like *Arminius, Die Standarte,* or *Die Kommenden,* that he had

published *Der Arbeiter* and *Die total Mobilmachung*, that he was connected to the "National Bolshevik" Ernst Niekisch. I also discovered the drawings of A. Paul Weber, who made a big impression on me. All this is well-known today, but at the time it was, for me in any case, completely new.

I hastened to communicate my discoveries. I returned repeatedly to the *Handbuch der Konservative Revolution*, while promising myself someday to publish a translation.[4] The first result of these efforts was the republication by GRECE (Groupement d'études et de recherche pour la civilisation européenne, the principal association of what was not yet called the New Right[5]) in the form of a small booklet of one of the rare texts already published in France on *Der Arbeiter*: Marcel Decombis, *Ernst Jünger et la « Konservative Revolution ». Une analyse de « Der Arbeiter »* (*Ernst Jünger and the "Konservative Revolution." An analysis of* Der Arbeiter).[6] The work of a dead Germanist, this text was augmented by a short bibliography and an original Foreword written by Armin Mohler, who presented

---

[4] That happened many years later, in the "Conservative Revolution" series that I edited for a few years: Armin Mohler, *La Révolution Conservatrice en Allemagne 1918–1932* (Puiseaux: Pardès, 1993). This translation, incorporating all the additions of the most recent German editions, included, moreover, an important album of photographs and an inventory of all the publications in France devoted to the Conservative Revolution. It is the only complete translation of Mohler's book published.

[5] The expression "New Right" was not initially a self-designation. It was invented by the media in 1979 to describe a current of thought that by then had already existed for more than ten years. This is why, conscious of the ambiguities that attach to it, I personally employ it as little as possible.

[6] Marcel Decombis, *Ernst Jünger et la « Konservative Revolution ». Une analyse de « Der Arbeiter »* (Paris: GRECE, 1973).

Jünger's work as "one of the rare great books of the century," but also as an "erratic bloc" within his works, and described its publication in 1932 as an "extraordinary occurrence." Speaking of *The Worker* and the first version of *The Adventurous Heart* (*Das abenteuerliche Herz*), he later said: "Today my hand still cannot pick up these works without starting to tremble."

In his Foreword, Mohler also said—with three repetitions—that *Der Arbeiter* was an "untranslatable" work. It did, however, end up being translated in 1989 by Julien Hervier,[7] without, moreover, really stirring up the polemics that Jünger had dreaded for some time.

At this time, I had not yet made Jünger's personal acquaintance. However, on May 15th, 1977, as I took part in the International Book Festival in Nice for both *Figaro-Magazine* and Éditions Copernic, which had a stand there (I had just received the Grand Essay Prize of the Académie française for my book *Vu de droite*), I intended to introduce myself. I turned around and saw a man of medium height, very straight, with a helmet of white hair, who wore a corduroy jacket over a fine turtleneck sweater. I did not recognize him at all. "Hello," he said, "I am Ernst Jünger." I was speechless. That day we talked for more than an hour. Photographs were taken. A great and beautiful memory.

Meanwhile, nearly ten years after the publication of the booklet of Marcel Decombis, I had collected enough documents regarding Jünger's youthful "political" period to write my own study of *Der Arbeiter*. The first version was published at the end of 1981 in *Eléments*,[8] then another,

---

[7] Ernst Jünger, *Le Travailleur*, trans. Julien Hervier (Paris: Christian Bourgois, 1989).

[8] Alain de Benoist, "La Figure du Travailleur. Réflexions sur un livre méconnu d'Ernst Jünger," *Eléments*, 40 (Winter 1981–82), pp. 13–19.

much longer version appeared two years later in *Nouvelle Ecole*.[9] The latter, which was followed by a translation of an article by Ernst Niekisch published in *Widerstand* in October 1932 ("Zu Ernst Jüngers neuem Buche"), was in fact a true monograph and was later published as a book in Spanish and Italian translations.[10] I made an effort not only to present the principal concepts of *Der Arbeiter* and to trace the author's development in the 1920s and 1930s by discussing some of the landmarks in the history of the national revolutionary movement, but also to show how the "problem of the Worker" continued to reappear in Jünger's later works, obviously in different forms, particularly the evolution of his ideas on technology under the influence of his brother, Friedrich Georg Jünger. I presented *Der Arbeiter* as indispensable to the understanding of the transitional period defined as an "interregnum" between the reign of the titans and that of the gods. I also made many references to the thought of Carl Schmitt and the philosophy of Martin Heidegger, with which I had then familiarized myself.

On March 29th, 1985, Jünger's ninetieth birthday, I sent him a telegram shortly after a public meeting in which I had taken part in Saint-Etienne. He thanked me with a short, handwritten letter to which a photograph was attached. Ten years later, on March 25th, 1995, I sent him a letter which contained only these words: "Thank you for being alive." To celebrate his centenary, the Club des Mille (the financial support association of the New Right) orga-

---

[9] Alain de Benoist, "Ernst Jünger: la Figure du travailleur entre les Dieux et les Titans," in *Nouvelle Ecole,* 40 (September-October, 1983), pp. 11–61. (Chapter 1, above.)

[10] Alain de Benoist, *Ernst Jünger y El Trabajador. Una trayectoria vital e intelectual entre los Dioses y los Titanes* (Madrid: Barbarroja, 1995); *L'Operaio fra gli Dei e i Titani. Ernst Jünger « sismografo » dell'era della tecnica* (Milano: ASEFI-Terziaria, 2000).

nized an evening in his honor on June 21st in Paris.

In 1996, I decided to devote a whole issue of *Nouvelle Ecole* to Jünger. The editorial that I signed there began with these words: "The twentieth century is the century when the Nobel Prize was not given to Ernst Jünger. That is as good a way to define it as any other." The issue included an interview with Jünger by his Spanish translator, Andrés Sánchez Pascual; essays by Armin Mohler, Gerd-Klaus Kaltenbrunner, Werner Bräuninger, Serge Mangin, Pierre Wanghen, and Marcus Beckmann; and translations of documents by Friedrich Hielscher, Albrecht Erich Günther, Ernst Niekisch, and Friedrich Sieburg.

Jünger seemed to have become immortal! At the end of 1997, I published a bibliography of his work with a publisher who was courageous (or unaware) enough to bring out that kind of book, which by definition would always find a rather restricted public.[11] This bibliography, with which I was not entirely satisfied, should have received a new, much-enlarged edition, on which I worked many years, but I finally gave up on it. Nicolai Riedel, the worthy successor of Hans Peter des Coudres and Horst Mühleisen, published his bibliography in 2003.[12] (Since then my work as a bibliographer has instead concentrated on Carl Schmitt.) At the beginning of my bibliography, I reviewed the main stages of Jünger's life. Reaching 1997, I wrote: "Having entered his 103rd year, he continues to write." Alas! A few months later, on February 17th, 1998, he died. I paid homage to him on March 7th in a Radio-Courtoisie broadcast.

---

[11] Alain de Benoist, *Ernst Jünger. Une bio-bibliographie* (Paris: Guy Trédaniel, 1997).

[12] Nicolai Riedel, *Ernst Jünger-Bibliographie. Wissenschaftliche und essayistische Beiträge zu seinem Werk (1928–2002)* (Stuttgart: J. B. Metzler, 2003). Nicolai Riedel regularly publishes updates of his bibliography in *Les Carnets Ernst Jünger.*

Since then, Jünger has been studied more than ever. On November 7th, 1995, I had already taken part in a Jünger conference organized at the La Sapienza University in Rome under the title "Due volte the cometa" ("Two Times the Comet," alluding to the fact that Jünger lived to see two appearances of Halley's Comet). I also took part in a large conference on Jünger held in Milan from October 20–24, 2000, where I had the occasion to make the acquaintance of Nicolai Riedel, the day before a concert of Ricardo Mutti at La Scala. At the end of a "pilgrimage" to the Chemin des Dames, I also attended a conference on Jünger and the First World War in Laon, on November 8th, 1998. Danièle Beltran-Vidal, François Poncet, Isabelle Rozet, Olivier Aubertin, Manuela Alessio, and some others also took part.

My admiration for Jünger—for the man and his work—has never faded. But perhaps it changed direction a bit. Thirty years ago, I was filled with enthusiasm for the "first" Jünger of the 1920s and 1930s. With time, and thus with age, I undoubtedly became more appreciative of the "second" Jünger—of the Anarch and even more of the Rebel, of the "timeless" thinker who, having risen higher, also sees farther.

I would like to add a very personal memory here. On February 6th, 1993, having been invited to take part in a debate in Berlin, I had the unpleasant experience of being physically attacked by a group of young "autonomous" militants advocating an archaic "antifascism" who did not even know that I had come to argue against xenophobia! Returning to Paris after a night spent looking at police photographs trying to identify my attackers,[13] I received a telephone call from Armin Mohler. He told me that Jünger, who had learned of the incident, immediately

---

[13] I recognized them perfectly, but I refused to say so. I do not collaborate with the police.

wanted to know about my condition. This gesture touched me greatly.

Ernst Jünger was probably not one of the authors most frequently quoted by the French New Right, but there is no doubt, as we have seen, that he was very much discussed. Today, there is no longer a need to "complete" Jünger's image in France. The various aspects of his work are now well known. Like Schmitt, Heidegger, and Mircea Eliade, Jünger was also, at one time or another, the object of critiques in the form of denunciations. They emanate from sectarian spirits that are not only anachronistic but deal with Jünger only in order to arrive at conclusions that fit the prejudices they had when they began. These approaches remain very much in the minority. Admittedly, Jünger is still seldom cited by fashionable intellectuals. One has to go to Italy to find intellectuals of all opinions, Left and Right, citing Jünger constantly (just as they also constantly quote Schmitt and Heidegger). But the readers of the author of *Eumeswil* and *Subtle Hunts* (*Subtile Jagden*) remain quite numerous.

Today, practically all Jünger's books have been translated into French; they are published by the largest houses; and most are constantly reprinted. The *War Diaries* (*Strahlungen*) have been republished by Gallimard in their prestigious "Pléiade" series, with an important critical apparatus by Julien Hervier, to whom we also owe a collection of conversations with Jünger.[14] Academic research is coordinated by the Centre de recherche et de documentation Ernst Jünger (CERDEJ), chaired by Danièle Beltran-Vidal, who since December 1996 has published an annual volume of *Carnets Ernst Jünger*. What is still needed is a complete translation of the political articles of his youth (these recently appeared in Italy, in three volumes) and of

---

[14] Julien Hervier, *Entretiens avec Ernst Jünger* (Paris: Gallimard, 1986).

the correspondence (especially the correspondence with Schmitt, Heidegger, Hielscher, Gottfried Benn, and Gerhard Nebel), but also a great "definitive" biography comparable with the one Heimo Schwilk recently published in Germany.

It is very curious that no book of Friedrich Georg Jünger has ever been completely translated into French. Taking into account his many connections in the publishing world, it seems that Jünger could easily have gotten some works of his brother published in France. For my part, it was a mistake that I never did anything. I often wondered why.

Ernst Jünger would be 110 years old today. "The silent revolutions are the most effective," he said. He should be read in silence.

INDEX

Numbers in bold refer to a whole chapter or section devoted to a particular topic.

59, 66, 67, 69, 76, 86,
102, 105, 136, 143
security, 28–29
Die Selbstherrlichkeit (Self-
Glory), 14
Seldte, Franz, 7
Shakespeare, William, 14
Shintoism, 95
Sicily, 19
"Sizilischer Brief an den
Mann im Mond"
("Sizilischer Brief an
den Mann im Mond"),
118
Sieburg, Friedrich, 159
Sievers, Wolfram, 15
Sinsheimer, Hermann, 47
socialism, non-Marxist, 28,
147; true, 28; compare:
National Socialism
Socrates, 127
Soldier, the, 32 **108–10**, 112,
115, 121; versus the Rebel
and Anarch, 116
solitary walker
(Einzelgänger), 69
Solomon, Ernst von, 13
Solzhenitsyn, Aleksandr,
54, 55
Sombart, Nicolas, 145
Sorel, Georges, 13, 60
sovereignty, 39, 45, 64; ver-
sus power, 114
Soviet Union (USSR), 51,
88. *See also* Russia
Die sozialistische Nation
(The Socialist Nation),
15
space, of work, 42, 44;
bourgeois, 42

Spartan life, 110
Spengler, Oswald, 9, 12, 14,
48, 61
spiritualization, 106
"stab in the back" *(Dol-*
chstoss), 7
Die Standarte, 5–6, 7, 13,
47, 155
Der Stahlhelm, 5
Der Stahlhelm-Bund der
Frontsoldaten (The
Stahlhelm Association
of Frontline Soldiers), 5–
7, 12
statism, 54, 68
Stapel, Wilhelm, 13, 47
state democracy
(Staatsdemokratie), 44
State within the State, 5
Stoffregen, Goetz Otto, 6
Stresemann, Gustav Ernst,
5
von Stülpnagel, Heinrich,
151
Subtile Jagden (Subtle
Hunts), 94, 161
Sturm (Storm), 8–9
Strahlungen (War Diaries),
161
Suddeutsche Monatshefte
(South German
Monthly), 18
suicide, 151–52

T
Tannenbergbund, 53
technology, 12, 17, 26, 29,
31–32, 35–36, **40–50**, 60,
62–63, **65–77**, 79–84,
87–88, 97–98, 101–13,

ABOUT THE AUTHOR

ALAIN DE BENOIST (b. 1943) is a political philosopher and historian of ideas. The author of a hundred books and thousands of articles, his recent books include *L'Homme qui n'avait pas de père. Le dossier Jésus* (*The Man Who Had No Father: The Jesus File*) (Krisis, 2021), *Survivre à la désinformation* (*Surviving Misinformation*) (La Nouvelle Librairie, 2021), and *Contre l'esprit du temps: Explications* (*Against the Spirit of the Age: Explications*) (La Nouvelle Librairie, 2022).

www.ingramcontent.com/pod-product-compliance
Lightning Source LLC
Chambersburg PA
CBHW031956010726
47493CB00007B/2226